THE ROYAL SCHOOL

Diaries

2

Lara's Leap of Faith

Written by Alexandra Moss

Grosset & Dunlap • New York

For Hannah Powell, who loves to dance—A.M.

Special thanks to Sue Mongredien

Series created by Working Partners Ltd

Copyright © 2005 by Working Partners Ltd. All rights reserved. Published by Grosset & Dunlap, a division of Penguin Young Readers Group, 345 Hudson Street, New York, New York 10014. GROSSET & DUNLAP is a trademark of Penguin Group (USA) Inc. Printed in the U.S.A.

Library of Congress Cataloging-in-Publication Data

Moss, Alexandra.
  Lara's leap of faith / written by Alexandra Moss.
     p. cm. — (The Royal Ballet School diaries ; #2)
  Summary: Ellie's first term at the Royal Ballet School is filled with excitement, hard work, homesick-ness, an unexpected chance to perform, and new friendships, tainted only by the rude and hateful behavior of Lara, the girl she crashed into during their audition.
  ISBN 0-448-43536-5 (pbk.)
  [1. Ballet dancing—Fiction. 2. Boarding schools—Fiction. 3. Schools—Fiction. 4. Interpersonal rela-tions—Fiction. 5. Royal Ballet. School—Fiction. 6. London (England)—Fiction. 7. England—Fiction.] I. Title.
  PZ7.M8515Lar 2005
  [Fic]—dc22
                                      2004021331

ISBN 0-448-43536-5   10 9 8 7 6 5 4 3 2

Dear Diary,

Well, here we are . . . my last night in Oxford. This time tomorrow I'll be in my new home . . . The Royal Ballet School's Lower School!!! I can hardly believe it.

So much has happened since Mom and I left Chicago a year ago. And to think that at first, I wasn't sure about coming to live in England! Now I'm so glad Mom got her job teaching here in Oxford. It has all worked out perfectly. If anyone had told me back then that I'd get a place at The Royal Ballet School, I'd never have believed it. A school where you dance every day, where you eat, sleep, and breathe ballet . . . I'd have thought that was too amazing to be true. Yet here I am, bags all packed, ready to start my first day there tomorrow!

It's nerve-racking as well as exciting, though. I really hope I make some good friends there. It's going to be awful saying good-bye to Phoebe and Bethany, my two best friends here in Oxford. I can't believe we've only known one another a year. It seems like we've been friends forever. I'll miss them sooo much.

I'd better get some sleep. Tomorrow is going to be one of the biggest days of my life!

I just realized I packed my pajamas already! Oops!

Ellie Brown gazed up at the beautiful white building as the car pulled up in front of it: White Lodge, home of The Royal Ballet School's Lower School. Located in the middle of Richmond Park in southwest London, the building was bathed in mellow golden sunlight that glinted off its huge windows. It was so awesome. And she was going to live there!

According to the school information pack she'd been sent—which Ellie had read so many times, she practically knew it by heart!—the building had originally been built as a hunting lodge for King George II in the 1720s. Other kings and queens had lived there, too—including Queen Victoria for a time. Gazing up at the lodge now, Ellie could easily imagine the kings and queens stepping out of their horse-drawn carriages and walking through the large double doors.

The building had became part of The Royal Ballet School campus in 1955. Today, the circular drive was filled with cars, with excited-looking girls and boys spilling out of them, clutching bags. Her mom and Steve, her mom's boyfriend, had brought Ellie here.

"You two go ahead," Steve told them. "I'll bring up the rear, with the heavy stuff."

Ellie smiled at Steve and felt glad all over again that he and her mom were now a couple. He was such a nice guy—and he always seemed to know when Ellie wanted some time alone with her mom.

Ellie's mom, Amy, got out of the car. "Now, honey," she said to Ellie, "will you let me hold your hand as we go in, or would that be just way too embarrassing for you?"

Ellie laughed. "I guess a little bit of hand-holding is okay today, Mom," she said, wrinkling her nose.

They each took a bag and strolled up to the front of the house. Ellie recognized a boy she'd seen at the Final Audition, looking embarrassed at the way his mom was hugging him. And there, climbing out of a taxi and gazing up at the school in awe, was the pretty dark-haired girl who had danced so incredibly that day.

A friendly-faced woman stood on the front steps, greeting everybody. "Mrs. Hall, housemother for the Year 7 girls," she introduced herself, her kind blue eyes on Ellie. "And you are . . . ?"

"Ellie Brown," Ellie told her.

Mrs. Hall ran a polished fingernail down a list on a clipboard. "Ellie Brown . . . Ah, here you are," she said, ticking Ellie's name off. "Very nice to meet you, dear. Just go through the double doors, and then follow the signs to the Year 7 girls' dorm. They're making so much noise up there already, you won't be able to miss them!"

"Thank you," Ellie said. She and her mom exchanged excited glances as they went inside.

As they stepped into the school entrance hall, Ellie shivered with delight. She'd been to the Lower School before, of course, when she'd had her Final Audition back in the spring. But the grandness of the building took her breath away all over again, just as it had back then. The hall was flooded with light from the large windows overlooking the driveway, and the walls were lined with framed pictures of famous dancers: Dame Ninette de Valois—who founded The Royal Ballet and The Royal Ballet School; Margot Fonteyn and Rudolph Nureyev; Antoinette Sibley and Sir Anthony Dowell; and Ellie's favorite—Darcey Bussell. Beautiful, ornate ballet costumes and ballet shoes were on display in glass cases alongside a long, polished wood reception desk.

"Wow . . ." Ellie's mom said in a hushed voice as their footsteps echoed through the hall. "It's like being in a museum."

"I know," Ellie replied dreamily. Her mind was already spinning, just thinking about all the world-class dancers who had lived and trained here before her. It seemed almost impossible that *she* was going to be studying here, too!

Through a second set of double doors was a smaller foyer, with corridors and a staircase leading off. There were a few other people coming and going through the foyer, but they all seemed to know where they were supposed to be. Ellie's mom looked across at Ellie. "I feel lost already," she joked. "Where did Mrs. Hall say we were to go?"

Ellie had rushed over to the bronze statue that stood a few feet before them. "Look, Mom, Dame Margot Fonteyn," she said breathlessly, and touched the middle finger of the statue's hand. "I remember this from the tour we had," she said. "Everybody touches Dame Margot's finger for luck. Quick, come and touch it, Mom!"

Her mom laughed but did as Ellie asked. The middle finger was worn silver where it had been touched by so many thousands of students over the years. "You don't need any luck, Ellie Brown," she told her daughter proudly. "You're going to be just fine. Now—where do we have to go?"

"Mrs. Hall said follow the signs," Ellie said, glancing around wildly. Then she saw a bright orange arrow pointing up the staircase. "Year 7 girls' dorm—THIS WAY!" it read.

Ellie and her mom went up the sweeping stone staircase that curved down to the hall. *Everything seems super-sized here*, Ellie thought to herself. The staircase was so wide, the ceilings were so high, the windows so large and light . . . She felt for a moment as if she were in an elaborate dolls' house, and she and her mom were teeny tiny dolls.

"Here we go," Mrs. Brown said, spotting another sign as they reached a first floor landing. Again, a couple of corridors led off from the landing, with rows of identical blue doors along each one. Ellie's head spun. Would she ever get to know her way around this place? she wondered.

She and her mom went through a small room with a piano and sofa in it—the Slip, Ellie remembered from her audition day tour—and then they were outside the girls' dormitory.

Ellie's mom pushed the door open. "What an amazing room!" she exclaimed.

Ellie nodded, suddenly lost for words, as they stood there in the doorway. The girls' dormitory was a long, thin, crescent-shaped room with large windows all the way along the curving outer wall. When Ellie had been here on the audition day, the students who lived there had hung up "Good luck on your audition!" signs everywhere, and it had looked really colorful and friendly, with ballet posters and photos covering the walls. Each girl's bed had had a bright, funky bedspread, and the shelves had been full of knickknacks and photos. Now it looked bare and empty, with the beds stripped and the shelves clear, but even that gave Ellie a thrill. She couldn't wait to start decorating her own space, to make it truly hers.

The beds were laid out under the windows with a wardrobe for each girl. They were arranged in two clusters—five beds toward the near half of the room, and six beds in the far end. The far end of the dorm room seemed to be full already. Someone had brought a small CD player, which blared out pop music. A girl with wavy auburn hair was pinning up posters and pictures above her bed. Someone's mom was smoothing out a bedspread, and someone else's little sister was running around squealing excitedly.

"Grace!"

"Ellie—thank goodness! Someone for this half of the dorm!"

Ellie beamed as her friend came rushing up to meet her. "Hi!" she cried happily. The two girls hugged each other. "Boy, is it good to see you again!" Ellie said, relieved to see a familiar face.

Ellie and Grace had met through Junior Associates—or JAs, as it was known. Every other Saturday they'd attended classes at The Royal Ballet School's Upper School building in the West End of London.

"You're in the bed next to me," Grace told Ellie, grabbing her hand and leading her along, as Ellie's mom followed them. "I've got Bed 3—and you're right here—Bed 4."

Ellie sat down on her new bed, which was under one of the high windows. Sunlight washed over her, warming her, as she gazed at her new surroundings. "Wow," she giggled. "My new bedroom, Mom!" She couldn't help thinking about her old room in Oxford, which had only one bed and just enough space for her things. It seemed so small compared to this great long bedroom she was going to be sharing with so many people!

"Isn't it enormous?" her mom marveled, gazing up at the ceiling. She strolled over to peer out of the window.

"Wow, we're really here, Grace," Ellie said, shaking her head in disbelief. "Do you feel as freaked out as I do?"

Grace nodded, tucking her long blond hair behind her ears. "I am *completely* freaked," she confided. "Excited, happy, scared . . . everything!"

"Oh—here comes the pack mule," Ellie's mom said, looking over affectionately to where Steve was walking in, bags slung around his shoulders. She turned to Ellie. "Now, honey," she said, "do you want us to stay a while and help you unpack—or would you rather us let you do that on your own?"

Ellie hesitated. Part of her wanted her mom and Steve to stay until the last possible minute. The other part of her was itching to get started with her new life. "I guess . . . I guess I'll do it myself," she said, a sudden catch coming into her voice.

Ellie's mom smiled, but Ellie could see tears in her eyes. "You're just trying to get rid of me before I start crying," she joked, pulling her close for a hug.

Ellie found she was suddenly unable to speak. She just breathed in her mom's perfume and wrapped her arms tightly around her neck. It had been just the two of them for so long and now Ellie and her mother were both going to be on their own! Well, not *really* on their own, Ellie realized, since her mother had Steve and *she* had the entire Lower School to keep her company! But what if her mother's multiple sclerosis flared up again? True, she hadn't had any attacks in quite a while, but it could come back at any point. Because of this, Ellie had been worried about going off to school and leaving her mom alone, but of course, Amy wouldn't stand for Ellie giving up her big dream. Sure Ellie was worried, but for now, at least she'd have to be strong—it was what her mom wanted, after all.

"Call me whenever you want to—about anything. Twenty times a day, if you feel like it," Amy went on, her voice muffled by Ellie's hair.

Ellie nodded. "Okay," she said.

Amy gave Ellie one last kiss and then let her go. "I'm so proud of you, honey," she said. "You're going to have a great time here, I just know it."

"You bet I am," Ellie said, trying not to cry herself. "Bye, Steve. Take care of Mom, okay?"

Steve gave her a hug. "You can count on it, Ell," he said. "I promise."

And then they were gone. As the door closed behind her mom and Steve, Ellie sat down heavily on her bed.

"Are you okay?" Grace asked.

"I guess," Ellie replied. Suddenly, she felt a little anxious about being here. She was so close to her mom—and now she was going to be living away from her for the first time in her life. She was glad of the distraction when the dorm door opened again and another girl came in. It was the dark-haired girl Ellie had seen outside.

"Hi, everyone," the girl said in a soft voice. She looked at the numbers on the beds and then went over to Bed 1, by the wall, where she opened her suitcase and began to unpack.

"Hi," Ellie called across to her. "I'm Ellie and this is Grace."

The girl smiled. She was stunningly pretty, with long black hair, golden skin, and almond-shaped dark eyes. "I'm Bryony," she said. "We were at the same audition, weren't we?"

"Yes," Ellie replied. "I remember you were awesome."

Bryony blushed. "I thought the same about you," she confessed. "Well, it seemed like everyone there was! I couldn't believe it when I heard I got a place."

"Me neither," Ellie said. The news from The Royal Ballet School had come as a shock—not only was the competition intense, but Ellie had thought she'd blown her chances, having crashed into another dancer during one of the routines. When she heard that she'd gotten in, she'd hardly been able to believe the news.

The dorm door opened again, and in walked another girl with her parents. "Hi, everybody!" she called breezily, a sunny smile lighting up her lively face. "I'm Sophie." She strode into the dorm as if she'd lived there half of her life. "Bed 2," she said to her mom. "Ahh—there we are!" Sophie flung her bags onto her bed and flopped down next to them. "Hey, guys, I hope none of you snores!" she said, grinning.

"Sophie . . ." her mom started saying warningly, but Sophie wasn't listening.

"Or what about sleepwalkers? I hope no one's going to sleep-walk over here in the middle of the night! Can you *imagine?*" She cocked her head thoughtfully. "I don't mind sleep*talkers*, though—especially if they come out with some secrets. Or—"

"Soph-ie!" her mom said, smiling. She looked over at Ellie, Grace, and Bryony. "I do feel sorry for you girls, having to share a room with this one. Talk, talk, talk, that's what you're going to have to put up with!"

They all grinned at Sophie, who put on a pained expression, then grinned back.

Ellie realized that all the beds were occupied now, except one: Bed 5, right next to her. Just then, the door opened again and a group of people came in. There was a tall, elegant red-haired woman and a round-faced, smiling dad with his arm full of bags, followed by two girls chattering to each other, and a little boy, with sticking-out ears and a cheeky, darting smile. Their lilting, musical accents caught Ellie's ear. They were Irish!

"Here we are," the woman said over her shoulder, as she set a small suitcase on the bed next to Ellie's. "Bed 5."

Ellie and the rest of the dorm watched as the family made their way along to the bed next to Ellie's. She watched with interest as the taller of the two red-haired girls heaved a sports bag onto her new bed—then Ellie gasped in horror as the new girl turned around. Oh, *no*! It was the girl she'd crashed into so clumsily at her Final Audition!

The red-haired girl looked over the other girls in her half of the dorm with interest. "Hi," she said warmly, "I'm Lara." Then her gaze alighted on Ellie, and her green eyes narrowed. "Oh," she said, with a sudden frostiness in her voice. "It's you."

Chapter 2

Ellie's cheeks flamed, and she got to her feet. "Um, yeah," she said, taking a step nearer to Lara. "Listen, I'm sorry about what happened at—"

Lara had already turned her back on Ellie and was talking to her family.

Not a great start, Ellie thought in dismay. Her skin prickled uncomfortably. Okay, so she'd messed up at the audition by crashing into Lara—but surely the fact that they'd both been accepted to the Lower School meant that it wasn't *such* a big deal. It wasn't like she'd wrecked Lara's chances, was it? And it *had* been a mistake!

Ellie sighed and turned back to Grace, Bryony, and Sophie. Sophie had just said good-bye to her parents and, rather than feeling remotely sad, seemed positively delighted about it. "How exciting is this, girls?" she whooped, throwing herself back on her bed and kicking her legs up. "Mum and Dad have gone— now we can start life at Lower School for real!"

Ellie grinned at Sophie's ecstatic face. "Don't you get along with your parents?" she asked curiously.

Sophie rolled over onto her side and propped herself up on one elbow. "Yeah, totally," she said. "They're great. It's just . . . *this* is going to be even better. I've got a brother—but I always wanted to have a sister too. And now . . ."—she waved her arm toward the far end of the dorm—". . . I've got ten of them!"

Ellie smiled but couldn't help feeling a little nervous, too. As an only child, she was used to having her own space. Going from no siblings to TEN was quite a jump! She couldn't imagine what it was going to be like.

Grace giggled. "Sophie—you're meant to be saying what an honor it is to be studying at The Royal Ballet School, and how you can't wait to become a 'bunhead'—you know, one of those ballet-obsessed people who eat, sleep, and breathe nothing but ballet!"

Sophie twisted her mouth down comically. "Oh yeah, that as well," she said airily. She stretched her top leg high in the air and pulled it over her head gracefully. "Oof," she muttered, "not so easy to do that in jeans."

Bryony was hanging up a baby-pink leotard, the ballet uniform for their year, and she patted it happily. "Wait until we're all wearing these on Monday, and dancing in one of those gorgeous studios," she said dreamily, doing a half-*pirouette* in her sneakers. "I reckon that'll be enough to turn me into a bunhead!"

Ellie hugged her knees up under her chin. "I can't wait to start dancing here, for real," she agreed.

"Me too," Grace said. "Hey—have you seen our timetable yet? It's pinned up on the wall there. Mrs. Hall said we're all going to get a copy later today."

Ellie, Bryony, and Sophie rushed over to have a look. Lara was still deep in conversation with her family.

"Wow—ballet every morning," Bryony read aloud. "Heaven, heaven, heaven!"

Ellie ran a finger along Monday's lessons. ". . . followed by . . . oh, help, math from eleven-fifteen until twelve. Then lunch, then geography, then drama, then English, then tuck . . . What's tuck?"

"I think that's when you get to open your tuck box," Sophie said. "We all get one, remember? It's where you keep all your goodies. I've got about sixteen chocolate bars in my suitcase, plus jelly babies, crisps, and . . ."

Ellie laughed. "You're going to need a tuck *room* to fit all that in, Sophie," she said. "I guess you could always donate a few spares to my box, if it won't all fit in yours . . ."

Sophie put her hands on her hips. "Nice try," she said, "but I'm not falling for a lame trick like *that*!" She looked curiously at Ellie. "You've got to be a wily Scorpio, trying to pull a fast one like that," she guessed.

Ellie grinned. "Nope, I'm an Aries."

"Oh, cool!" Sophie beamed. "I'm a Leo—we get along just fine, us fire signs." She turned to Grace and Bryony. "How about you?"

"I'm a Virgo," Grace offered.

"Aha. A perfectionist," Sophie replied. She glanced over at Grace's tidily arranged belongings and whistled. "Should have guessed that, Grace!"

"And I'm a Cancerian," Bryony said.

"Just like my best friend at home," Sophie said happily. "That's okay. I'll be kind to you, you sensitive little crab, you!"

While the others were giggling, Sophie turned back to the timetable. "So what's after tuck? Is that the end of the day?"

"No chance," Bryony said, shaking her head. "On Monday, it's a character dancing class, then supper, then free time, then bed."

"Character class—we'll get to dance with the boys," Ellie said. "That'll be fun."

Grace pulled a face. "As long as I get a partner who's taller than me this time," she moaned. "Remember in JAs, Ellie? I usually ended up dancing with Archie Dent, who was like . . ."—she held her arms open wide—". . . this much shorter than me. Talk about an odd couple!"

Ellie nodded with a grin. "What else have we got?" she wondered aloud, running a finger along the timetable. "Swimming on Tuesday, choreography on Wednesday, gymnastics on Thursday and . . . Dal—what's that on Friday? Dalcroze?"

"I was wondering about that, too," Grace said. "Do you think it's a misprint?"

"Maybe it's code for 'hour off to hang out in the common room,' " Sophie said hopefully.

"I think it's kind of a music lesson," said Bryony. "You have to dance to different rhythms . . . And stuff like that . . ." she finished vaguely.

"Ri-i-ight," said Sophie, sounding doubtful. "Clear as mud!"

"It's a busy old week, anyhow," Grace said, her eyes scanning down the rest of the timetable. "We're going to need a holiday by the weekend!"

Sophie did a little *pas de chat* back toward the beds. "Is it just me, or does being here seem like a really weird dream?" she asked.

"It's not just you," Ellie replied as she and Grace went over to sit on Grace's bed. "I feel like I'm in a dream too—the best dream ever!"

Bryony went and sat next to Sophie. "I was at a boarding school before coming here," she told them, pointing her toes. "I had a message to say I'd got into The Royal Ballet School during lunch one day. I screamed so loud that three hundred girls turned round to look at me."

The others laughed.

"What about you?" Sophie called over to Lara. Lara's family had just left after a round of embraces, and Lara was sitting on her bed, with her back to them. "Lara, isn't it?" Sophie went on. "How did you feel when you found out you were coming here?"

After a brief pause, Lara turned and smiled at Sophie. "Oh, I was thrilled!" she replied. Then she threw a cool little look at Ellie. "I could hardly believe it, though—after what happened at the audition, I mean."

Sophie raised her eyebrows. "Oh? What happened?" she asked.

Lara tossed her long red hair back from her face. "Someone tried to make me look bad in front of the selectors," she said, shooting another sharp look at Ellie.

Ellie felt her cheeks burn at the way Lara told it. It hadn't been like that! Of *course* she hadn't bumped into Lara on purpose! But what if Lara told everyone that it was Ellie and they all believed her story?

Luckily, Sophie was distracted by Lara's accent. "Wow—we're a real mixture here, aren't we?" she commented. "Lara's Irish, Ellie—you've got to be American?"

Ellie nodded. "From Chicago—but I moved to Oxford last year."

Sophie turned to Bryony. "How about you?" she asked.

Bryony smiled. "My mum's from Singapore, my dad's Irish— and I was born in England. Not sure what that makes me!" she laughed.

"Exotic, that's what!" Sophie replied. She shrugged. "Sorry to let the side down, guys, I'm just from boring old England— Manchester, to be precise."

"Me too," said Grace. "Basingstoke."

"I suppose we should finish our unpacking," said Bryony.

Everyone nodded and turned their attention to their cases and bags.

Ellie looked at Lara. She really wanted to smooth things over—and fast! It was awful to have made an enemy of one of her new classmates already—especially one she was going to be sleeping next to! Lara was now putting up posters and arranging photos on her shelves.

"That's a good idea," Ellie said chattily. "I've got some photos to put up, too. I've got some of our vacation—Mom and I went to—"

"Really," Lara said in a chilly voice, cutting Ellie off before she could finish.

Ellie's mouth shut with a snap. With a heavy heart, she turned away and emptied out the rest of her packed clothes onto the bed. Somehow or other, in the short time since she'd left home, she seemed to have completely blown it.

"It's almost one o'clock!" came a voice from the doorway, and there was Mrs. Hall's smiling face at the door. "Before we have lunch, could everybody gather in the Slip so I can run through a few things with you?"

Ellie, Grace, and the rest of the girls followed Mrs. Hall out of the dorm and into the Slip, a small room between the dorm and the corridor. There was a sofa in there, plus a piano, a bunch of lockers, and a notice board.

"I know you probably feel completely overwhelmed right now," Mrs. Hall began with a smile, "but you'll be amazed how quickly you'll settle in. Now, I'm sure you've all seen the timetable pinned up on the dorm wall—do go and have a look at it if you haven't already done so. I'll be giving you each your own copy later today. Of course the timetable for this, your introductory weekend, is rather different. So here's what's in store for you today: after lunch, a treasure hunt has been arranged for you and the Year 7 boys. It's always fun—and will help you get to know your way around the school a little better," Mrs. Hall explained with a smile.

"What's a treasure hunt?" Ellie whispered to Grace, who was squeezed in next to her on the sofa.

Grace explained that it was a game in which various teams competed to be the first to collect all the items on a list they were given, usually for a prize.

Ellie realized with a smile that a treasure hunt was the same as a scavenger hunt—as they called it in America.

"Tomorrow, the rest of the school will be arriving," Mrs. Hall continued. "You'll get a chance to meet your guides in the afternoon—I take it you all know about the school family system?"

Feeling another thrill of excitement, Ellie nodded with everyone else. To help them settle in and feel at home, every Year 7 student was assigned a "guide" from Year 8 and a Mum (for girls) or a Dad (for boys) from Years 10 or 11. Ellie's guide was named Jessica—and Ellie had received a really friendly card from her over the summer, telling her what a great place Lower School was, and how much fun Ellie would have there. Ellie was really looking forward to meeting her.

Mrs. Hall then ran through some rules. "Just to remind you, you're not allowed to go off campus unaccompanied at any time," she said, her warm blue eyes serious now. "We arrange shopping trips for you at the weekend, and days out occasionally, but you'll be chaperoned with a teacher. That's very important—please don't wander off alone. What else? Phones! You're all allowed to have one at school—as long as you switch them off while you're in classes, and at lights-out, too. Which is nine o'clock. Laundry! There's a laundry rota pinned up on the notice board there— you'll be taking it in turns to take the dorm laundry to and from the laundry room, where it'll be washed and ironed for you."

She paused for breath. "Finally . . . I want you to think of me as a friend, as well as your housemother. I know nobody is as good as your real mum, but if you feel ill, or homesick, or just plain down in the dumps, please come and find me—my room is right next to the Slip here. And believe me, I've been here for so long, I've heard it all before. I am completely unshockable!"

"There's a challenge," Sophie joked, and everyone laughed.

"Right, well, that's enough serious stuff for now," Mrs. Hall said with a smile at Sophie. "We'll catch up again tomorrow evening before school starts for real, so if there are any questions you want to ask me, you can ask them then. But now—lunch!"

A cheer went up around the girls. Ellie hadn't realized just how hungry she was. She'd barely been able to touch her breakfast that morning, she'd been so excited!

They followed Mrs. Hall out of the Slip and down the stone staircase to the foyer again, then farther down to a long, arched red-brick tunnel. Ellie and Grace grinned at each other in excitement. The tunnel had a cavernous feel to it—and Ellie was reminded of Alice following the white rabbit underground in *Alice in Wonderland.* "Down the rabbit hole . . ." she muttered to Grace.

Grace laughed. "That is *exactly* what I was thinking!" she cried.

"Nearly there," Mrs. Hall said, turning around to make sure everybody was still behind her. "Right—now that we're at the end of the tunnel, you make a sharp left—and here we are!"

Ellie smiled to herself in relief. *Well,* that *hadn't been so difficult to find,* she thought.

"Now, just to warn you—there are *two* of these tunnels in White Lodge, and everybody gets them muddled up at first! Don't worry. You'll soon get the hang of it," Mrs. Hall assured them. She stood to one side and waved them through to the dining room. There was a pile of trays and, straight ahead, a counter serving hot food. "Help yourselves," Mrs. Hall said. "There's always a selection of hot dishes just here, and a salad bar further along the counter. On your right, there's a pasta bar where you can help yourselves to pasta and whatever sauce you fancy."

The girls all took trays and started helping themselves. Ellie decided to have a slice of quiche, new potatoes, and some of the salads.

"Where are all the puddings, that's what I want to know?" Sophie whispered behind her. "I can't survive without dessert!"

"Me neither," agreed Bryony.

Suddenly more voices and the clatter of feet could be heard. The Year 7 boys were coming! Ellie felt a smile break over her face as she spotted Matt Haslum, a friend from her JA classes. She waved excitedly at him.

"Ellie!" he shouted over the din. "Fancy seeing you here!"

"I can't believe they let *you* in," Ellie joked.

She and Matt had always been partners for the character dancing part of their JA classes until his family had moved farther north. After the move, Matt's nearest JA class had been in Birmingham. Ellie had missed him. Character dancing hadn't been the same without her funny, gossipy friend.

"Once you've got your food," Mrs. Hall said over the chatter, "I suggest you make yourselves comfortable at these tables here." She pointed to the first line of tables in the seating area, nearest to the food. "It's not a fixed rule by any means, but the tables at the far end of the canteen are usually taken by the older students." She smiled kindly. "I wouldn't want any of you to feel like you were in the wrong place when the rest of the school gets here."

Ellie sat down next to Grace and Matt and started eating. There were so many things to remember! Would she ever feel like she truly belonged here?

*   *   *   *

After lunch, it was time for the scavenger hunt.

"You've all had a tour of the school, but it will take a while for you to really get to know your way around," Mrs. Hall told them. "Most students get lost here in the first few weeks—so you might as well enjoy yourselves while you do so today!" She gave them all a wink. "And there's a treasure at the end, for everybody who manages to get there!"

There were eleven boys and eleven girls in Year 7. The boys' housemother, Mrs. Randall, told everyone to get into groups of four or five. Ellie, Grace, and Sophie immediately huddled together. Bryony grabbed Lara and joined them.

Mrs. Randall passed out the clue sheets. "Good luck, everyone!" she said, smiling. Then she started sending teams out at five-minute intervals.

When it was their turn, Ellie and the rest of her team pored over their first clue.

I'm iron and gray, I hang from a wall.
Now I am silent, but once I could call.

"Once I could call?" Ellie repeated. "What does that mean?"

"What calls?" Grace pondered. "A phone? A mouth?"

"There's a pay phone in the corridor near our dorm," Sophie said. "Maybe it's out of order now so you can't call on it. Could that be it?"

"It says 'iron' though," Bryony pointed out. "Iron and gray," she muttered, her pretty forehead creasing.

"It sounds like it's something old," Ellie said, thinking aloud.

"Well, *duh*," Lara snapped. "Everything's old in this place, isn't it?"

Ellie stiffened. Lara didn't have to be so rude about it! "I only meant—" she started crossly, but Sophie was running ahead.

"Let's just start looking!" she called impatiently.

The girls followed Sophie into a warm, sunny corridor and then outside into a cobbled courtyard.

"Where are we?" Ellie asked, putting aside her irritation at Lara as she gazed around. The courtyard was enclosed on three sides by old brick buildings.

"It's the academic wing, where the regular classrooms are," Bryony reminded her. "I think it used to be the old stable block, you know, where the king's horses were saddled up."

"Wow," Grace breathed. "This place has such an amazing history."

Ellie looked around the courtyard at the buildings that had been converted into classrooms. Though they were regular rooms now, she could still imagine the horses' hooves clip-clopping over the cobblestones outside, could almost smell the sweet scent of hay and . . .

Sophie was laughing. "What idiots we are!" she cried. "It's right under our noses—look!"

Ellie blinked and turned to look at where Sophie was pointing. There was an old gray bell attached to the wall on their left.

"Iron and gray . . ." Bryony smiled. "Very good. Is there another clue there?"

Lara was first over. "Yes!" she cried.

"Read it quick," Sophie ordered. "I think I can hear the next group coming!"

Lara cleared her throat and read:

Some people think I'm a dessert,
But I was a great dancer, too.
Just find the studio with my name
To get to your very next clue!

Ellie's mind raced. There was a Margot Fonteyn studio, wasn't there? And . . .

Sophie beat her to it. "The Pavlova studio!" she laughed. "Dessert—get it?"

Ellie frowned. Even though she'd been in Britain for a year, she was still surprised sometimes by all the British things she didn't know about yet!

"A pavlova—you know, meringue and fruit and cream," Grace told her, licking her lips. "Mmmm, delicious!"

The rest of the scavenger hunt was really fun. The clues took them around the large, light dance studios, back to the academic block to one of the science rooms, to the small indoor swimming pool that was tucked away off one of the corridors, outside to the biggest tree in the school grounds and then to the cozy library. By the end of the afternoon, Ellie felt like she was starting to get to know her new home a little better. And best of all, the last clue led to a "treasure chest" of chocolate coins!

"Just have a few each," Mrs. Hall told them. "It'll be supper soon. Which reminds me, if you've brought any food with you, bring it to me after tea and I'll show you where your tuck boxes are. You can get food out of your tuck boxes twice a day—at four in the afternoon and again at quarter past eight each evening. I'm sure you've all read your Lower School information packs but just to remind you—there's no food allowed in the dorms."

A few people groaned at that, including Sophie. Ellie guessed that Sophie had already stashed away some of her goodies in their dorm!

After supper, the Year 7 girls went to check out their common room, which they'd be sharing with the Year 8 girls, who would be arriving tomorrow.

Sophie whistled as they went in. "Niiiiice!" she cheered.

"Awesome," Ellie agreed. She sank happily onto the enormous plum-colored sofa.

"What a cool room," said Grace, excitedly checking out the cupboard full of arts and crafts equipment. "There are paints, sewing stuff, beads, glue, glitter pens . . . wow!" she said. "Are any of you guys good artists?"

Ellie laughed out loud, remembering how her friends in Oxford had always teased her about her terrible artistic ability. "Afraid not," she confessed. "Dancing—yes. Painting—no."

Bryony curled up on the sofa, tucking her dainty feet underneath her. "How did you guys get into ballet anyway?" she asked.

Sophie answered first. "My mum says I've been a show-off since the day I was born," she told them. "She reckons almost as soon as I could walk, I was putting on shows for her and Dad, and anyone who'd watch me. There are all these old photos of me tottering around in Mum's heels, trying to do high kicks and . . ." She stood up and did a little dance like a wobbly toddler, sending all the others into fits of giggles.

"I was like that, too," Ellie confessed. "My grandma took me to see *The Nutcracker* when I was three and I was just hooked. I got a video of it for Christmas and drove my mom nuts, asking to watch it again and again, trying to copy the steps . . ." Ellie still adored the magical story of Clara and the nutcracker doll. Even though she'd watched the ballet zillions of times, Ellie always got a thrill when the nutcracker doll turned into a soldier prince and took Clara on the magical journey to the Land of Sweets!

"The same happened to me," said Bryony. "Only with me, it was *Swan Lake*. I wanted to be Princess Odette when she's been turned into a swan. Still do, actually. All those *fouettés*!" She jumped up and started whirling around.

"My mum got me into ballet, I suppose," Grace said, leaning back comfortably on the sofa. "She was a good dancer herself— but she stopped when she married Dad, and had me. She used to help me practice around the living room for hours—you know, it was our special Mum-and-Grace thing." She looked a little home-sick suddenly, Ellie thought. "I think she was even more excited than me that I got a place at The Royal Ballet School!"

"How about you, Lara?" Bryony asked.

"My cousin Fiona got me interested," Lara replied. "We did

Irish dancing at school, which I loved, but we had to wear these awful clumpy shoes for it." She grinned at Bryony. "Not the funkiest things to wear on your feet! And then my mam and dad took me to Fiona's Christmas show—she was this great big girl of—ooh, at least ten, whereas I was this skinny little six-year-old. There she was in this pink fluffy tutu and shiny pink ballet shoes, and I was just . . . Wow. After that, Fiona never heard the end of it. 'Aww, Fiona, will you show me that ballet again, will you?' " She grinned again and flicked her hair over her shoulders. "It's a shame red hair clashes so badly with pink, but you can't have everything your way, can you?"

As each of her new dorm-mates talked about how she'd gotten to where they were all now, students of The Royal Ballet School, Ellie felt a rush of happiness. It was so *awesome*, she thought, to be with classmates who were all as crazy about ballet as she was. Sure, her friend Bethany, from ballet school in Oxford, had understood how much Ellie loved to dance—but some of the girls at her regular school hadn't. In fact, one girl had been pretty mean to her for a while, calling her Princess Tippitoes and other stupid names. *I fit in here*, Ellie realized. *They're all as crazy about ballet as me!*

It felt great. No, better than great. It felt like she had come home.

Dear Diary,

I'm writing this on my new bed . . . in my new dorm. Yes—I'm really here at The Royal Ballet School. It's starting to feel less like the craziest dream ever, and actually starting to seem real.

It's been a hectic day. I can't take it all in. All these new faces . . . trying to find my way around the school . . . saying good-bye to Mom . . . I can't believe it's only twenty-four hours since I last wrote in this journal. It feels like a whole year!

I'm writing this by the light of my mini flashlight because I'm too wired to sleep. My head is buzzing! Mrs. Hall came in ages ago— nine o'clock—to put the lights out. It is so weird having somebody do that. "I know you're excited, girls," she said, "but tomorrow's another big day so try and get some rest."

Somehow everybody else seems to be managing that except me! We were all whispering and giggling for ages at first, until Mrs. Hall came back in.

"Gi—irls," she said. It was dark, but you could tell from her voice that she was smiling. "Try and get some sleep now. You don't want me phoning your parents and saying, 'Oh dear, your daughter can't get to sleep—maybe she's not ready to live away from home,' do you?"

There was this huge gasp of shock—I mean, we all know she wouldn't really do that and she was only joking, but even so . . . the thought of having to go home . . . It shut everybody up pretty fast. And now nobody's saying anything!

My mind is racing too much to switch off yet. And it's so noisy in here! Someone is snoring further down the dorm. Somebody's got a clock that ticks really loudly. And I can hear Grace breathing next to me as she sleeps. I guess I'll just have to get used to sharing a bedroom. Either that, or I'll have to get earplugs . . .

I'll write more tomorrow. Right now, I must try and get some zzzzs—and switch off this light before Mrs. Hall comes in and catches me!

Signing off,
Ellie Brown, Year 7, Royal Ballet Lower School!!!!!!!!

"Good morning, girls!"

Ellie blinked as the room was flooded with light. She rolled over and pulled the pillow over her head, still groggy with sleep.

Wait a minute . . . who'd said that? That wasn't her mom—and she wasn't at home!

Her eyes opened fully underneath the pillow. Mrs. Hall! She was at The Royal Ballet School! It was like waking up on Christmas morning, suddenly realizing that something special was happening. She sat up and looked around, rubbing the sleep from her eyes. Wow. She was really here!

"What are you grinning about so cheerfully, Ellie?" Sophie called over from where she was still snuggled under her duvet. "Oh, no, don't tell me you're one of those super-happy morning people, are you?"

Ellie snorted. She'd never been called *that* before! Back home, her mother practically had to drag her out of bed for school. "Absolutely not," she told Sophie. "You can call me a lot of things, but not a morning person!"

Bryony poked a head out from under her covers. Even first

thing in the morning, she looked neat and tidy, with her hair still sleek and silky, rather than sticking out everywhere like Ellie's usually was! "How did you all sleep?" she asked, yawning delicately.

"Terribly," Grace said, stretching her arms above her head. "Who was it, snoring like a road-drill all night? Did you hear it, Lara?" she asked, as Lara walked by to the bathroom.

Lara shook her tousled red hair out of her eyes. "Can't say I did," she replied. "Mind you, I'm used to sharing a room with my sister—who snores like a trooper! I could sleep through just about anything!"

"We'll blame the girls at the other end of the dorm," Sophie decided, pulling on a dressing gown and grabbing her toothbrush and towel. "None of us five could possibly make such a noise!"

The girls all washed and dressed casually, either in jeans and T-shirts, or their new red school sweat suits. Then they went downstairs for breakfast. Ellie couldn't stop yawning. She hoped it wouldn't take her long to get used to sleeping in a dorm with ten other people. Otherwise she'd never catch up on her beauty sleep!

After breakfast, the students had "free time" where they could do as they chose. "Anybody fancy a game of football?" Matt said, jumping up and pretending to head an imaginary ball outside the canteen. "Lads? Girls?"

Lots of the boys thought this was a good idea. So did Ellie. She liked soccer—or football, as everyone called it in the UK. She had played it at school back in Chicago and it was very popular over here. "Do you want to join them?" she asked the other girls.

Grace and Bryony weren't keen. But Sophie said she'd play, as did Lara, who told the others that she'd played on the soccer team at her old school. And two girls from the other end of the dorm—Kate and Rebecca—said they'd play too.

Ellie tied her hair up in a ponytail and followed the boys outside. At the back of the house was a large grassy area. A fence marked the edge of the Lower School grounds; on the other side was the vast space of Richmond Park.

A tall dark-haired boy called Oliver, who Ellie knew from JAs, volunteered to count everyone off into two teams.

The game got off to a lively start—ballet dancers were quick on their feet! Ellie was on a different team from Lara and Sophie.

"Hey!" Ellie called after Lara came at her, with both feet out, sending her flying to the ground for the second or third time. "Watch it!"

"Are you all right, Ell?" Matt asked, grabbing one of her hands and pulling her to her feet.

"Yeah," Ellie said. "I'm okay." She shook the mud off her jeans crossly as she watched Lara score a cracking goal between the two goalposts. *It's only a game*, she reminded herself. *Keep your cool.*

Lara was very good. Annoyingly good, Ellie thought to herself crossly. Even some of the boys were raising their eyebrows at one another, as if they were surprised that a girl could play their beloved game so well.

Moments later, Lara and Oliver were passing the ball neatly to each other again, then Lara glanced up at the goal, saw she had another clear run, and headed up the field.

Ellie raced after her. Lara wasn't going to have it all her own way! She swerved in front of Lara and tried to kick the ball away from her. But as her foot touched the ball, she found herself skidding on a muddy patch and ended up on her butt—sending Lara tumbling over, too.

"Foul!" shouted Lara furiously, her eyes blazing. "Deliberate foul!"

"Sorry," Ellie said, getting to her feet and holding out a hand to pull Lara up. "I didn't mean to—"

Lara cut her off sharply. "You're making a bit of a habit of this, Ellie Brown," she said accusingly, ignoring the hand that Ellie was offering. She stood up, glaring in annoyance at the streaks of mud on her sweatpants. Her green eyes were murderous.

"Honestly, it was an accident," Ellie said. She felt mortified. *Oh, great,* she thought glumly. *Now I've just made things even worse!*

"That's what you said about the last time, too," Lara said scornfully. "And I didn't believe you then, either." She tossed her red ponytail and ran back up to where Oliver had the ball.

Matt had seen the whole thing. "Ouch," he said sympathetically. "She doesn't like you much, does she?"

"No," Ellie replied bluntly. "She doesn't. Even less now, I bet."

Ellie watched Lara jog over to her teammates. She didn't feel like playing anymore. Luckily she was saved from any further run-ins when, moments later, a shout went up.

"They're here! The older students are arriving!"

"Looks like the game's over," Ellie murmured, seeing Sophie and the others drift around the front of the school to see the new arrivals. She couldn't help feeling a bit relieved. She had an inkling that Lara was going to bear an even bigger grudge against her now—for what had been an innocent accident. Clearly, she wasn't the type to forgive and forget easily.

After she'd taken a shower and changed into clean clothes, Ellie joined Grace and Bryony at the dorm window where they were watching the older students arriving. They all looked so happy to be back—bursting out of cars to run over and hug one another, squealing and jumping up and down excitedly.

"That'll be us, this time next year," Bryony said.

It was a strange thought. Ellie could hardly imagine it. Getting through the first week at her new school seemed enormous in itself, let alone getting through the first year!

Grace was peering at one of the girls. "I think that's Maria— my guide!" she said. "She sent me a photo. See her, there, pink tracksuit top and ponytail?"

"I can't wait to meet Jessica," Ellie said, looking out of the window. "I wonder if she's out there now? I've got no idea what she looks like."

"My guide's called Kelly," Bryony told them. "She phoned me up over the summer. She sounds *so* nice. She—"

Mrs. Hall popped her head around the door just then. "Lunchtime, girls," she reminded them.

Ellie jumped. Lunchtime again, already? The morning had flown by without her even noticing it.

Now that the whole school was present, the dining room seemed a whole lot noisier than it had the day before, Ellie thought, once they'd made their way there. The line of people waiting to get food snaked right out of the doors. All the other students were chatting away to one another about their holidays, their ballet, their news. Suddenly Ellie was reminded just what a new girl she was, and felt shy. All these older, taller, more confident students seemed really intimidating. Even talkative Sophie was quieter than usual.

After lunch, there was a short welcome speech from Mr. Knott, the Head of the Lower School. He greeted the new students and said how lovely it was to see the returning students looking so fit and healthy. Ellie caught a few mumbles and guilty chuckles at that, and she wondered if all the students had been self-disciplined enough to practice right through the holidays—or not!

Then it was time for the Year 7s to get together with their guides and Mums or Dads. Everyone gathered in the assembly hall and the housemothers read out the names of the Year 7 students one by one.

When Mrs. Hall read out her name, Ellie found that she was holding her breath. She saw two friendly-looking girls make their way toward her and let it out again.

"Hi! I'm Jessica, your guide!" said the younger-looking girl, who had a broad smile and thick dark hair tied in cute bunches. She gave Ellie a hug.

"Welcome to Lower School!" said the older girl, giving her a hug too. "I'm Hannah—your Lower School Mum."

"Hi," Ellie said, smiling back. For some reason, she was blushing wildly. There was just something about the older students that made her go all shy!

The two girls led Ellie over to a corner of the room to chat.

Jessica handed Ellie a bag. "Here, I made these for you—kind of a good-luck tradition here," she said, her brown eyes twinkling.

Ellie opened the bag and drew out its contents. She gazed in delight at the pair of old pointe shoes that Jessica had decorated with colorful sequins, beads, and ribbons. They were so pretty! "Thank you!" she cried. "I feel luckier already!"

Jessica and Hannah laughed.

Ellie looked up again at Hannah. For some reason, her willowy frame, long fair hair, and pretty, freckled face seemed very familiar. "Have we met before?" Ellie asked. "I'm sure I recognize you . . ."

A rose-pink blush spread across Hannah's skin. "Um . . . I'm on the front of the school Annual Report this year," she told Ellie. "So it's probably just my photo you've seen."

Idiot! Ellie thought to herself. She'd goofed already, and she'd only just met Hannah!

"Hannah won the Young British Dancer of the Year award last

year," Jessica chimed in proudly. "Everyone reckons she's a definite for Upper School next year, don't they, Han?"

Ellie's mouth fell open. "Wow," she gulped. Of course! She was *that* Hannah! She'd read all about the competition in the school magazine she'd been sent.

Hannah rolled her eyes. "Not that Jess is putting pressure on me or anything . . ." she laughed. She turned to Ellie. "How are you finding Lower School, so far? Are you settling in okay?"

"Yes, thanks," Ellie said, her voice little more than a whisper. "I love it here already." All she could think was, Young British Dancer of the Year . . . wow! Her "Mum" was a celebrity!

"It's strange at first, isn't it?" Jessica said knowingly. "We all remember that mad first week, not knowing where you're going . . ."

"Missing your home," Hannah put in. "Worrying that every-one's going to be a better dancer than you . . ."

"Exactly," Ellie told them, relieved that they seemed to understand just how she felt. "There's so much to take in. And I feel so lost!"

Jessica put a comforting arm around her. "Don't worry," she said. "We've all been there. And you can come and talk to us about anything. Anything at all!"

"Thank you," Ellie said, in awe of these older, more confident girls. Jessica was just a year older than she was, but she seemed far more relaxed at Lower School than Ellie thought she'd ever feel.

. . . .

That evening, Mrs. Hall called a quick dorm meeting in the Slip. Ellie squeezed herself onto the sofa, along with Grace, Sophie, and Kate. Lara and Bryony shared the piano stool, and the others crowded together crosslegged on the floor.

"I just wanted to check that everybody's all right so far," Mrs. Hall started. Everyone nodded as she looked from face to face. "I know it's strange at first, being here," she went on. "Some of you might be missing home already, and wondering what you've let yourself in for. But I'm sure once you've had your first ballet class, you'll start to feel a bit more at home." She broke into her usual cheerful smile. "So best of luck for tomorrow, all of you. And finally . . . I hope that wasn't a torch I spotted last night, when I peeped around the dorm door at nine-thirty? Lights-out means lights out!"

Ellie felt her cheeks grow bright red. Oops! Caught! She'd better not try that one again, she decided—not if she was going to stay on Mrs. Hall's good side, anyway!

"I'll be around for an hour or so if there's anything you want to talk to me about," Mrs. Hall finished. "Otherwise, see you all at lights-out."

"Anybody fancy a game?" Sophie suggested, jumping up off the sofa. "I saw some in the common room. Shall we check them out?"

Grace, Bryony, and some of the other girls thought that was a good idea, but suddenly, Ellie found herself longing to call home—to speak to her *real* mom.

"I'm just going to make a call," she told the others, heading back to the dorm to pick up her cell phone. "I'll catch up with you later."

"Honey! I was just thinking about you!" her mom cried happily once the connection went through. "How are you? What have you been doing?"

As Ellie told her mom everything, she imagined her sitting in her favorite chair at home, bare feet tucked up underneath her as usual, coffee cup somewhere close by. It was comforting, yet kind of sad at the same time. She knew her mom so well—they had been such a tight twosome of a unit ever since Ellie's dad had died when she'd been a toddler—and now, here they were, in separate buildings, in separate cities. Ellie wouldn't get to be a part of her mother's everyday life, or even see how she was doing with her MS. Ellie realized that there were a lot of changes she was going to have to get used to, now that she was living at The Royal Ballet School.

Dear Diary,
    I've found a private spot outside, on a stone balcony overlooking the back garden. It's getting kind of dark and chilly, but I'm all bundled up in my fleece and there's an outside light so I can just about see well enough to write. It's kind of nice anyway,

seeing the park getting darker and darker in front of my eyes. Really reminds me that we are truly in the middle of nowhere!! It is so beautiful here, though—really awesome to be surrounded by miles of open parkland! Bryony reckons she spotted deer trotting around out there, through our dorm window this morning. How cool is that?

I just spoke with Mom and now I feel a bit homesick. It didn't hit me how much I'm missing her until I heard her voice. I miss Phoebe and Bethany in Oxford, too. I must e-mail them soon—and everybody in Chicago, as well, of course: Heather and Libby—and Grandma and Gramps!!

I feel like I've made some good friends here already. Grace is lovely, of course, and Sophie is great fun—and Bryony seems really nice. And then there's Lara . . . I hope things get better between her and me. She seems to get on with everybody else just fine.

Tomorrow's a big day—the first day of term. First ballet class in the morning. Yippee! I can't wait to dance again. I'm looking forward to seeing how everyone else dances, too. I know Grace is amazing, of course, but I can't help feeling curious about Sophie and the rest of them. Bryony seemed so good at the audition—and actually, Lara did too—when I wasn't knocking her over . . . I just hope I'm not the worst dancer there anyway. I guess I'll know soon enough!

Chapter 4

"This is taking ages! My toes are getting cold!"

Ellie tried not to giggle at Sophie's whisper. It was Monday morning and they, along with the rest of the Year 7 students, were sitting barefoot in the light, airy Salon, waiting to have their feet measured for new ballet shoes. The huge Salon windows gave breathtaking views of the grounds and the grand pathway that led out into Richmond Park.

"I'll be here at the start of every year, and at the end of spring term to measure your feet," Mrs. Gourlay, one of the shoemakers, had told them. "I'll measure the width and length, obviously, plus what we call the 'vamp,' which is the distance between the tip of the shoe to the elastic."

At last, it was Sophie's turn to be measured. Mrs. Gourlay ran her fingers over Sophie's feet and moved them gently. "I think you're going to need something a bit special," was her pronouncement.

Sophie winked at Ellie and the others. "Great! I'm special!" she said.

"Yes," Mrs. Gourlay went on, "because you don't have the most flexible feet I've ever seen, my dear." She smiled sympathetically up at Sophie. "Let's think, what would be a good make of shoe for you?"

"Oh, right. *That* kind of special," Sophie said, sounding less enthusiastic. "My old ballet teacher said my feet had rather flat arches." She pulled a face. "She showed me some exercises that I could do to build them up."

Mrs. Gourlay nodded. "And your teacher was absolutely right," she said, patting Sophie's foot gently before scribbling down some notes. "Not to worry. You'll just have to work extra hard."

Sophie wrinkled her nose in dismay. Ellie could tell she didn't like the sound of that!

"The physio here will be able to help you with the exercises," Mrs. Gourlay said, as if she hadn't noticed. "Lots of dancers do extra exercises to strengthen their feet. These things can be made up for with willpower."

Grace was next. "Good strong feet," Mrs. Gourlay said decisively. "And what long toes you have!"

Grace blushed. "My mum calls them 'monkey toes,' " she confessed, which made everyone giggle. "She reckons I'd be good at swinging from branches with them."

Mrs. Gourlay chuckled too, as she jotted down Grace's measurements. She measured Bryony next. "A nice, neat foot," she said approvingly, writing down a few more notes. "All in proportion—one of the easy ones. Now who's next?"

Lara obligingly stuck a foot out. "What a beautiful foot," Mrs. Gourlay said, admiring the arch. "Absolutely lovely-looking but . . ."

"I know, I know," Lara said gloomily. "Banana feet. I've heard it all before, Mrs. Gourlay. It runs in my family."

Mrs. Gourlay took Lara's foot. "It *is* a high instep," she agreed. "Beautiful to look at, and wonderfully flexible. But you'll have to work hard on your feet, like Sophie."

"I know," Lara said, with a shrug. "I do exercises that my ballet teacher gave me, but maybe I should talk to the physio too?"

Mrs. Gourlay nodded. "I think so, dear," she said. "And take heart—dancers who look after fine flexible feet like yours often go on to be brilliant leapers—it's the great *spring* you have in those feet, you see?"

Lara smiled and nodded, looking happier.

Then it was Ellie's turn. "More nice, neat feet!" Mrs. Gourlay said happily. "They feel very strong—and what splendid square toes, my dear!"

Ellie blushed. Her JA teacher, Ms. Taylor, had said that a ballerina should ideally have her big toe, second, and third toe of similar length, so as to spread the weight across all toes when dancing on pointe. Ellie had already known that her feet were strong—but it was still nice to have a professional say so.

Then she caught the scowl on Lara's face at Mrs. Gourlay's words and felt a twitch of annoyance. It wasn't *her* fault that she didn't have problem feet, and Lara did!

"Quite a narrow width," Mrs. Gourlay went on, and pursed

her lips. "Let's see . . ."

Ellie enjoyed having Mrs. Gourlay pull out a range of different shoes for her to try. Mrs. Gourlay really seemed to care that everyone had the perfect fit.

Once everyone had been measured, the girls all ran to the dorm to change into their ballet clothes. Their first ballet lesson started in only ten minutes!

"I just know I'm going to fall over," Grace wailed, smoothing out a crease in her leotard.

Ellie pulled her sweatpants over her leotard and looked across sympathetically. Even though Grace was a very good dancer, she did seem to get nervous. "Don't worry, I'll be there with you," she told her. "Right on my butt, knowing my luck."

"That'll be a change," Lara muttered in a low voice to Bryony. "Usually she's the one knocking *other people* over."

Ellie spun around indignantly, and Lara gave her a cold look.

"Watch out, Ellie," Sophie joked. "Lara's a Scorpio. And you shouldn't cross a Scorpio. They just *have* to get revenge!"

Sophie seemed to think that Lara was referring to the tumble she'd taken in the soccer match, but Ellie knew differently. "Revenge for what? I knocked you over by *accident*!" she protested. "Everyone makes mistakes, don't they?"

"Hey! Who's having a go at Scorpios?" came a voice from farther down the dorm. It was Megan, a Scottish girl. "Cos I'm one, too, you know!"

Sophie winked at Ellie. "See? Don't mess!" she whispered.

"Nothing, nothing, Megan," she said in a louder voice. "We just love Scorpios down here. Don't we, Ell?"

Ellie caught Lara's eye and shrugged.

"I was told it's not such a terrible thing to fall over now and again," Bryony said, playing peacemaker. "Everybody does it—even the professionals."

Sophie, all ready to go with her sweat suit over her ballet things and sneakers on her feet, began twirling merrily around the room, swinging her ballet shoes from one hand.

"Sophie, how can you be so calm?" Grace called over to her.

Sophie carried on twirling, her sneakers squeaking on the floor. "I'm a Leo, remember!" she called back. "Can't you tell? We love performing. Born show-offs."

"What are Leos like at hairdressing?" Ellie asked, grimacing at her reflection. Her fine hair was usually on the wispy side, but today it seemed fluffier than ever. "Anybody know how to do a bun?"

Bryony picked up a water-sprayer and waved it in the air. "This is the secret weapon," she said. "Want me to show you?"

"Yes, please," Ellie said gratefully. She watched in the mirror as Bryony sprayed her hair with a fine mist of water and combed it straight back. Then she scraped it into a ponytail and curled it neatly around and around inside a bun net.

"There," said Bryony. "Easy as that."

"Wow," Grace said admiringly. "Where did you learn that?"

Bryony bent down to tie her sneakers. "I just . . . you know, picked it up somewhere," she said vaguely. "I can't remember."

"Get a move on down there," Megan called suddenly as she and Holly walked down to the door. "Class starts in five minutes!"

Ellie saw that Lara was still only half-dressed, with her red hair still tumbling down to her shoulders. The Irish girl looked panicked at the time check and started scrambling into her sweatpants.

Ellie hesitated, and then said, "Want me to help you with your hair?" Okay, so she'd only just learned how to do it herself, but still . . . it was a peace offering, wasn't it?

Lara didn't even look at her. "What and have you jabbing hairpins in my head? No, thank you very much," she said tightly. "Bryony, would you be a doll and help me?"

Ellie's heart sank. "Suit yourself," she said stiffly, snatching up her ballet shoes as kind Bryony went over to help Lara. "Come on, Grace."

Ellie, Grace, and some of the others ran through the Slip and down the stairs. As they passed through the entrance hall, each of them rushed over to the statue of Dame Margot and touched her lucky middle finger. They needed all the help they could get before their first formal ballet class at Lower School—everybody wanted to dance better than they'd ever danced in their lives!

"It's in the Ashton Studio, isn't it?" Sophie asked, glancing around the different corridors that led off from the hall. "Anybody know where to go?"

"I think it's through that tunnel," Kate said decisively. She sounded so sure of herself that they all followed.

The girls raced along the low brick tunnel. Lights were strung overhead, but Ellie had that cramped, underground feeling again as she went through the long tunnel that snaked through the school. It was odd, not being able to see any glimmering of daylight and, even though she knew for a fact it was almost eight-thirty in the morning, being in the tunnel made her feel as if it could very well be the middle of the night!

Kate came to a stop and frowned. "I wonder if we've come through the right tunnel?" she said suddenly, sounding a whole lot less certain.

The other girls stopped abruptly too. "I'll ask in here," Ellie said, going up to a half-open door on one side of the tunnel. She peeped around the doorway, only to gasp in delight. On the other side of the door was . . . an Aladdin's cave of brightly colored costumes hanging from the ceiling and rails all around the small room. "Wow," she breathed. "Grace, come and see. This must be the wardrobe department!" She could see pink silk and silver capes and what looked like a sea-green ball gown, spangly turquoise bodices, jeweled headdresses, and . . .

"Hello, girls!" a pleasant voice said as Grace and Sophie both joined Ellie in curiosity. "I'm Jean, the wardrobe mistress. Are you lost, by any chance?"

Ellie smiled at the friendly-looking woman, who'd emerged from behind a rack of dresses. "Yes," she said. "We're looking for the Ashton Studio—are we going the right way?"

The wardrobe mistress shook her head. "Afraid not," she told them, sounding amused. "Go back to where you started then follow the tunnel in the opposite direction, past the laundry room. The glass door at the end leads to the Ashton Studio. You can't miss it."

"Sorry, guys," Kate panted, as they ran back the way they'd come.

"At least we're getting a good warm-up," Sophie said.

．　　　．　　　．　　　．

In the Ashton Studio, once they'd eventually found it, there was a small, athletic-looking woman waiting for them. She was leaning against the piano, talking to the pianist, but as soon as the girls started coming through the doors, she stood up straight and regarded them with interest. "Good morning," she said, in a clear, musical voice.

Then the door opened again, and Lara and Bryony rushed in, looking a bit flustered. Ellie guessed that they'd gotten lost, too.

The teacher counted heads and then gave a little nod. "So, we're all here," she said, smiling. "My name is Ms. Wells. I'm going to be your ballet teacher for the whole of your first year," she told them. "We'll start by going right back to basics for the first few lessons—practicing all the exercises as if you've never done them before, in order to get everyone familiar with The Royal Ballet School's way of doing things." She put her hands on her hips. "So, let's begin with some warm-up stretches."

Ms. Wells arranged the class into three rows. Ellie was in the middle row, between Grace and Sophie.

"Shoulders up and down first," Ms. Wells said, "up to your ears, high as you can . . . and down. Up to your ears, high as you can . . . and down. Now let's roll our heads around to warm up the neck muscles . . ."

Ellie felt herself relaxing. It was great to be back in a ballet studio—especially here! Her ballet school in Oxford, the Franklin Academy, had closed over the summer months and there hadn't been JA classes over the summer either. Ellie had had to practice at home instead, or with her friend Bethany. It hadn't been the same thing at all as real classes.

Next it was barre. "You'll see it's a double barre in here," said Ms. Wells. "Tall girls—you can use the top barre. The rest of you, use the lower barre."

Ellie tried both and felt that the lower barre was more comfortable for her, but some of the other girls—including Grace—were tall enough for the higher one.

Once barre exercises began, Ellie started to realize just how out of practice her body was. To her relief, from the muttered groans she could hear around the studio, she wasn't the only one to feel that way.

The exercises seemed to go on forever! When, at last, they came to an end, Ellie's forehead was wet with sweat and her legs were all wobbly.

"Good work, girls," Ms. Wells said. "Time for a stretch, now. Left leg up on the barre."

She took them through an exercise Ellie had done before. With the left leg on the barre, they had to bend the right knee down, down, agonizingly down, and then straighten it and rise up onto the right tiptoes. Then they had to stretch the left arm over the left leg.

"Slide your leg along the barre, and off . . ." Ms. Wells said, demonstrating, "turn, right arm out to the side, and . . . slide down into the splits. And give me a smile while you do it!"

Ellie felt her muscles throbbing at the stretch. She gritted her teeth with the effort of smiling, as Ms. Wells walked around, correcting positions.

After more stretching, and then some center work, Ms. Wells said, "Let's have a look at your jumps now—*sautés*, everybody!"

The girls went back into their rows and the pianist started to play a jaunty tune. "And . . . first position," Ms. Wells said. "Shoulders open, tummy strong, arms relaxed. And . . . *sauté. Sauté. Sauté*. Keep going. Lovely, Lara. Keep pulled up, Megan. *Sauté. Sauté. Sauté*. Land *quietly*, Sophie."

Lara was in the row in front of Ellie. Ellie had been concentrating so hard on her own ballet that she'd barely glanced at anybody else, but she couldn't help noticing how high Lara was jumping. Her legs seemed to be like springs, sending her effortlessly high. Then Lara's head turned slightly to the side and she caught Ellie looking at her. With a proud toss of her head, she launched herself higher still.

Ellie gritted her teeth and willed herself to jump as high as

Lara. She'd manage it even if it killed her to do so!

.   .   .   .

By the end of the class, every single girl was red-faced and sweaty. Ellie's heart was pounding, her arms and legs ached from being stretched and pulled, and her hair was all over the place.

"Well done, all of you," Ms. Wells said warmly. "I'm impressed. Now you can have a hot shower. You've earned it!"

"I can hardly walk," Sophie groaned as they filed out of the studio. "I thought we were going back to basics! That seemed like really hard work!"

"It was, wasn't it?" Ellie agreed, wiping the sweat out of her eyes. "I loved it, though. Wow—and we're going to be doing that every single day!"

"It sure beats schoolwork," Bryony said happily.

Grace grinned. "Yeah, but we get that *next*," she reminded her. "Math's in fifteen minutes, remember?"

Sophie clapped her hands to her face. "Noooo! Have we really?" she cried.

"Sophie Crawford," Ellie teased in a mock British accent, "I do believe you haven't been checking your timetable." She was joking, but she was also exhausted. Having ballet *and* regular school every day was going to be a challenge, that was for sure!

The girls ran up to the dorm to shower and put on the school uniform. It was the first time they'd all worn the green and blue plaid skirts, white blouses, and navy blue cardigans, and Ellie and Sophie got the giggles about how proper they all looked.

"Now, where do we have to go this time?" Grace wondered as they grabbed their school bags and supplies, and left the dorm.

"Don't ask Kate," Ellie teased, "or we'll end up in Richmond Park!"

"I know where to go," Lara said, striding ahead briskly. "It's near the computer room. Just off the little courtyard, remember?"

"And how do you know where the computer room is?" Sophie wanted to know as they followed Lara down the stairs. "Not a computer nerd as well as a super-duper leaper, are you?"

Lara grinned over her shoulder at Sophie's comical expression. "As if!" she snorted. "No, I've been going there to send e-mails," she said. "My family are all missing me like crazy already," she laughed. "I've got to write to the poor darlings to keep them going."

Lara took them through one of the tunnels—the one with the Aladdin's cave of costumes—and out into the cobbled courtyard. It was just starting to rain as they clattered across the cobblestones and into the academic block. "Here we are," Lara said proudly. "Look—the boys are here already."

The girls filed in and sat down quickly. The classroom was small and cozy with a chalkboard at one end, and brightly colored posters with mathematical problems all over the walls. Matt gave Ellie a wink and a salute as she sat down with Grace, and she waved back.

"Hello," the man at the front of the classroom said. "My name is Mr. Best, and I'm going to teach you all about the wonderful world of mathematics."

A couple of people groaned, and Mr. Best smiled. "Heavens, do you mean to say, I don't have a class full of dedicated mathematicians?" he exclaimed, throwing up his hands in mock horror. "Ahh, we'll soon change that. You'll all be fraction fans by the time I've finished with you. They don't call me 'Best' for nothing, you know!"

This time everyone groaned at his joke and he started handing out new exercise books and math textbooks for each student, and Ellie and Grace elbowed each other, trying not to giggle. Somehow, it felt more difficult than ever to settle down to a serious math lesson, when just twenty minutes before they'd been *pirouetting* in a ballet studio!

"I know what some of you are thinking—what do fractions have to do with ballet, anyway?" Mr. Best said, turning to chalk up some figures on the board. "Well, here's what. Imagine there are six ballerinas each wanting to practice for four hours a day, but there's only enough room in the studio for five of them to practice at any one time." He grinned and looked around at everyone. "How many hours will it take for all of them to get their practice done?"

The class was silent. "At this point, I am meant to be hearing the gentle rustling of paper as you all open your exercise books and start working out the answer," prompted Mr. Best. "Who's going to be first to tell me the fraction you need to work out in order to solve the problem?"

Ellie took the lid off her pencil tin and took a pencil thoughtfully. She'd never even dreamed of studying math in relation to ballet before. It had always been just . . . a bunch of numbers before. But when she thought of those same numbers in terms of ballerinas—well, suddenly, it seemed a whole lot more interesting!

To Ellie's surprise, the lesson passed quickly. They worked out the number of *sissones* a dancer would have to jump in order to cross a ten-meter studio, if each *sissone* spanned exactly one meter, twenty-five centimeters. And they calculated the total length of a barre, if it had to run around a studio that measured ten meters by fifteen meters. Ellie was in the middle of working out a problem that involved calculating the number of leotards required for the school, when the bell rang for lunch. She was so engrossed in the puzzle that Grace had to shake her. "Hey! Keen bean! Time to eat," Grace said.

It was only then that Ellie realized just how hungry she was. All the exercise she'd done that morning had made her ravenous— again. And as she got to her feet, she was reminded just how hard she'd been dancing. Every single muscle in her body was throbbing!

"Thank goodness it's lunchtime," she joked to Grace as they scuttled through a light drizzle across the courtyard again. "I'm starving! I feel like I've already done a full day's work here, don't you?"

Grace was frowning. "Where's the dining room again?" she asked.

"I've got absolutely no idea," Ellie confessed. Then she giggled. "I can see you and I are going to be star students when it comes to geography, Grace," she joked. "Let's just hope we're studying a map of the Lower School this afternoon!"

Dear Diary,

I am stretched out on my bed, so sorry if I doze off. I danced so hard this morning, my legs are still aching! I hope they're going to toughen up fast, otherwise I'll need a cane by the end of the week!

Today was my first real day at The Royal Ballet School . . . wow. It felt awesome to dance here. I think I did okay. I didn't mess up and do anything too dumb, anyway. Everyone here is really good, though. Bryony is brilliant. And Grace, too, of course. Amazing Grace! I'd forgotten how she can make even the most basic plié look totally elegant. And Lara—well, her dancing is great too—but boy, is she being annoying! She really doesn't like me—and won't let me even try to make things right. It's her problem, Grace says—but she's turning it into my problem, too, when she bites my head off the whole time.

I called Mom after dinner tonight. It's a really warm evening so I sat outside, in the cobbled courtyard to speak to her. She couldn't believe it when I told her I was sitting right where the king's hunting horses used to be stabled!

She wanted to know all about my day, and it was nice to catch up. When I'm not busy, like now, I miss her a lot.

I think some of the other girls here are homesick too. I woke up in the middle of the night and heard somebody crying, but I'm not sure who. Sophie is sending tons of text messages to her mom and friends, desperate not to miss out on any gossip from home, she says. Grace has already decided to go home this weekend because she's worried her dog, Harvey, is going to miss her!

Bryony and Lara seem okay though. Bryony is used to being away, I guess, having boarded at her previous school. And Lara never talks about being homesick—though it seems like her family and friends in Ireland miss her a bunch—she spends ages answering all their e-mails and cards and stuff. I guess she must be nice to them!

Better go—just time to write a quick birthday card to Heather in Chicago before it's lights-out! I am soooo not going to get caught by Mrs. Hall tonight!

Chapter 5

After a few days, Ellie realized that life was settling into a pattern. The lights were switched on with a cheerful "Good morning, girls!" every day at seven o'clock. Then there was a bleary-eyed rush to get washed and dressed for breakfast. The hot breakfasts had fast become Ellie's favorite meal of the day. She always had a bit of everything: eggs, bacon, sausage, baked beans, toast. It gave her plenty of energy for dancing, she figured!

Ellie loved the two-hour morning ballet class with Ms. Wells. They were still going through fairly basic positions and movements, but Ms. Wells made them push harder, stretch further, reach higher than Ellie had ever done before. It was exhilarating to feel her body working so hard. Already, she wished Mrs. Franklin could see just how much she was improving. She knew her old ballet teacher would be proud of her.

On Friday afternoon, Ellie arrived at the studio for her first Dalcroze lesson, still unsure quite what to expect. They had been asked to wear just a leotard, with bare feet.

Ms. Malone, the teacher, was waiting for them in the studio. "Dalcroze eurhythmics was first developed in the early 1900s by a

Swiss musician and teacher named Emile Jaques-Dalcroze," she told the class. "It's all about understanding music through movement. We'll listen to different musical rhythms—then you'll express them in dance terms. It's about interpreting the music *your* way, creating your own movements."

The whole class stared blankly back at her, and she laughed and turned to the pianist. "Mrs. Cox, if you'd be so kind?" she asked, and the pianist played a series of notes.

"And again, please, Mrs. Cox?" Ms. Malone asked.

Once the pianist had finished, Ms. Malone clapped her hands to the rhythm of the notes. "DAH-DAH da-da-da," she hummed. "Slow, slow, quick, quick, quick. Everybody got that?"

Ellie nodded, feeling intrigued.

"Good," said Ms. Malone, "because I'd like you to split into twos and threes now. Then I want you to put together a series of movements to that rhythm. Slow, slow, quick, quick, quick. Slow, slow, quick, quick, quick. Okay?"

The class broke into small groups and started whispering and stepping through movements. Ellie was with Grace and they both had ideas.

"How about we start opposite each other, and mirror each other?" Grace suggested.

Ellie swished her foot out to the side. "Maybe start with a *glissade*?" she wondered aloud. "And go into some *sautés*?"

They tried to fit the slow, gliding movement of the *glissade* into the rhythm. All around, girls were muttering, "Slow, slow, quick, quick, quick!"

"That's lovely," Ellie heard Ms. Malone say. "What did you say your name was again, dear? Lara? Well done, Lara. You've got great rhythm!"

Ellie tried not to make a face. Lara, Lara, Lara. Every teacher seemed to single out Lara for praise! She wouldn't mind if it were anybody else in the class—she'd be pleased for them!—but when Lara was still being so unfriendly and cold toward Ellie, there was a part of Ellie that wished Lara would fall over every now and then, or do something wrong.

After Dalcroze, the girls showered and dressed for supper. "Hooray for supper," Sophie cheered, zipping up a sweat suit top, her hair still wet. "Who's coming with me?"

"Try and stop me," sighed Grace, pulling on her shoes hurriedly. "I saw on the menu that it's pizza tonight."

"Pizza!" cried Bryony happily, patting her tummy. "I could eat three!"

Grace glanced over to Ellie, who was still half-dressed. "Want me to wait?" she asked.

Ellie laughed. "I wouldn't dare keep you from your pizza, Grace."

Grace and the others went racing downstairs, leaving only Ellie and Lara in the dorm. Lara didn't seem to be in a hurry to eat; she was engrossed in something she was writing, lying flat on her stomach on her bed. Lara had been getting cards and letters every day from Ireland, and seemed to be writing home every spare minute she got.

Ellie finished tying her sneaker laces and straightened up. She was just about to leave the room, but she felt awkward. If it had been anybody else lying there, she'd have waited for her to finish so they could go to supper together. But as it was Lara . . . why should she bother?

She turned to go, but felt uncomfortable doing so. Ellie's mom had always been strict about good manners, and thinking about other people. She could almost see the look of disapproval on her mom's face, at the thought of Ellie leaving Lara without saying anything.

She sighed. "Are you coming to supper, Lara?" she asked tentatively.

Lara turned her head and glared at Ellie. "Can you not see I'm in the middle of something here?" she demanded.

"All right, all right," Ellie said, getting to her feet. "No need to be like that. I only said . . ."

"I heard what you said," Lara said, turning back to her letter.

Something snapped inside Ellie. "Lara," she said crossly, "what is it with you? Why do you always have to be so rude to me? It's not still because of what happened at the audition, is it?"

"What, when you tried to push me over? When you tried to wreck my chance of getting a place here?" Lara's eyes were fierce. "Not to mention when you tried to break my leg at football the other day. How could I possibly bear a grudge about that, hmmm?"

Ellie groaned in exasperation. "It was a *mistake!*" she cried hotly. "A dumb mistake! Get over it, Lara! You got your place at Lower School, didn't you? And I *didn't* try to break your leg in football. I slipped! I just *slipped!*"

She marched out of the dorm before Lara could reply, anger bubbling inside her. Lara was just so *maddening!* Why did she have to be so prickly about everything? She couldn't exchange two words with Ellie, without launching into a full-scale attack!

Ellie banged the door behind her. She was wasting her time with Lara. She'd tried, hadn't she? She'd tried many times, in fact. And look where trying had gotten her!

Ellie ran down the steps to the canteen. As quickly as it had flared up, her fury was subsiding. Now she was starting to feel a little annoyed with herself. She'd flown off the handle with Lara, when she'd wanted to straighten things out. She knew exactly what Sophie would say about *that.* "That's because you're a hot-headed Aries, Ell. You talk before you think!"

It was true. She hadn't handled things very well back there with Lara. In fact, she'd just made everything ten times worse. She jumped down the last few steps, angry and distracted, and almost went flying into Matt.

"Ellie Brown—do you call that a *sauté*?" he teased.

Ellie felt a rush of relief to see his friendly face. "I'm so dedicated, Matt, I just can't stop practicing," she joked back.

Out of the corner of her eye, she suddenly saw Lara coming down the stairs. She did not want to get stuck sitting next to her in the canteen! "I'm starving," she said quickly. "Coming to get some dinner?" She spotted Justin, one of Matt's friends in the line. "Justin won't mind if we squeeze in with him, will he?" *Anything to avoid getting stuck next to Lara!* she thought.

Dear Diary,

I'm writing this just before I go down to the computer room as I've got a whole stack of e-mails to write to people tonight—Pheebs, Mom, Bethany, Grandma . . . This week has gone so fast, I'm getting behind already!

This is just a quick entry because Sophie's booked the school pool table for a competition in a little bit—Year 7 girls versus Year 7 boys. Obviously we're going to wipe the floor with them!

Anyway, it's Friday night and the end of the first week. Time has just flown by! In some ways, I feel like I've been here for ages. I'm getting used to waking up here now, used to having breakfast with one hundred people, rather than just Mom. I'm even getting the hang of where everything is. I didn't get lost once today!

Things are still terrible with Lara and

me. We had an explosion tonight where I lost my cool and shouted at her. Well, it feels like I've been biting my tongue forever, and I just couldn't help it. She is so rude and stubborn! I wish I didn't have to sleep next to her every night. Ms. Wells gave me a "Well done" for my developpés today. I went bright red, I felt so happy—but Lara had this scornful look on her face, like she thought she was better than me, or something. She's one of those dancers who can get her legs around her ears without even trying. Well, watch out, Lara—I'm right behind you!

I got a letter from Mom today. Sounds like things are going better and better with Steve. They're going away together next weekend, hiking. Six months ago that would have made me feel jealous, like he was taking her away from me. Now, though, I think, good for her! She went all those years without dating anybody after Dad died. I feel like she held out for the right one all that time, and here he is, somebody special. She sounded so happy. And that makes me happy too.

Oops—better shut this journal up fast. Lara has just walked in—and glared at me of course. She'd be glaring at me worse than ever if she knew what I'd just written about her. . .

Chapter
6

"I've got exciting news this morning, girls!"

Ellie and the rest of the class turned to Ms. Wells expectantly.

"As some of you will already know, every year, The Royal Ballet puts on a Christmas performance at The Royal Opera House in Covent Garden," she explained. "And this year it's *The Nutcracker.*"

Ellie held her breath, waiting to hear what was coming next. Were they all going to be taken to see the show?

"Each year, some of The Royal Ballet School students are given small character roles to dance in the show," Ms. Wells said, and Ellie couldn't help but let out a gasp. Was Ms. Wells about to say what Ellie thought she was? That they weren't just going to *see* the performance—that they might actually *dance* in it?

Ms. Wells's eyes crinkled at the corners as she smiled at all the excited faces before her. "We have two student casts, who will alternate the performances," she went on. "That means twice the number of opportunities!"

Sophie's hand went up at once. "Which parts are they, Ms. Wells?" she asked excitedly.

"Not the leading role of Clara, I'm afraid, Sophie, if that's what you were hoping for." Everyone laughed—including Sophie. "We need party guests, though—and flowers, dolls, mice, toy soldiers, gingerbreads, a rabbit drummer . . . all sorts of small character roles."

Ellie could hardly breathe, she was so excited at the thought of dancing on stage with The Royal Ballet . . . at The Royal Opera House . . . in *The Nutcracker*! Wait till her mom heard about this!

"Due to time pressures, there won't be formal auditions for every part," Ms. Wells went on. "Instead, the casting directors will sit in on some of your lessons this week, to see you dance, and then make their decisions."

Ellie's heart beat even faster. *This week?* It was all happening so fast!

"Which lessons will they be coming to, Ms. Wells?" Grace wanted to know.

Ms. Wells gave her a reassuring smile. "I'm not sure myself yet, Grace," she said. "The teachers haven't been told either. But you don't need to worry about it. Just do your best, all of you— and try to forget there's anyone else in the room." She clapped her hands at that point. "Right! That's enough talking! Let's get you warmed up and dancing!"

There was a buzz of whispers around the room as the girls made their way to the barre. Ellie really hoped she had a good week this week! She *so* wanted a part in *The Nutcracker*. Talk about a dream come true!

The excitement had spread right through the school. Nobody could talk about anything other than *The Nutcracker*, and which part they hoped for. Ellie really wanted to be a party guest. She loved the bit where the party children arrived to see the Christmas tree being lit. It was so magical, and festive, and . . . well . . . just so . . . *Christmassy*!

Over lunch, Sophie kept joking that whatever Ms. Wells had said, she wanted nothing less than the part of Clara. "Wait until those selectors are in our class," she kept saying. "I'll do a double—no, a triple *pirouette*, right in front of them."

The others laughed at Sophie's confidence. Ellie wished she had some of it. Sophie was so totally and utterly sure of herself, even though technically, she wasn't the most accomplished dancer. In fact, of all of the Year 7 girls, it was Sophie who seemed to goof up most often, Ellie thought privately.

"What part are you hoping for, Lara?" Bryony asked, interrupting Ellie's thoughts.

"A party guest would be grand," Lara replied, her face animated. "My godmother took me to see *The Nutcracker* in Dublin a few Christmases ago. I loved seeing all the party children. It was my favorite bit."

Ellie was just about to exclaim, *me too*! Then she closed her mouth. What was the point of saying anything to Lara? She'd only get a rude reply.

"That's what you want to be, too, isn't it, Ellie?" Bryony said, turning to her.

"Yeah," Ellie replied. She couldn't resist a look at Lara who, of course, was pretending not to listen to her answer, as usual. Ellie smiled sweetly. "Let's hope there's room for both of us, right, Lara?"

Lara didn't reply, but Ellie could guess what she would be thinking. *I'm not sharing the stage with YOU, Ellie Brown—Royal Opera House or not!*

"I'd like to be one of the toy soldiers," Bryony grinned.

"How about you, Grace? What about the rat king?" Sophie joked.

Grace laughed—as did everybody at the table. The thought of gentle Grace as the horrible rat king was hilarious! "I'm not sure," she said thoughtfully. "I love that bit when Clara's in the Land of Sweets, you know the Dance of the Mirlitons? The dancing cream puffs? I'd love to do anything in that scene." Then she gave a shudder. "I'm not looking forward to having the directors in our lessons, though," she said. "Imagine! It'll be like auditioning for a place here, all over again!"

"You'll be fine, Grace," Ellie said. "Just block them out of your head. I've seen the way you focus in ballet lessons—you won't have a problem with that."

Grace smiled, but the smile didn't quite reach her eyes, Ellie noticed. She wondered why Grace was being so twitchy about it. Surely she must know she was one of the best dancers in their year? She was bound to get a good part, absolutely no questions asked!

• • • •

The very next morning, Ms. Wells had just told the girls that she wanted them to dance a sequence of steps across the studio, one by one, when the door opened, and two people walked in. Ellie's heart almost missed a beat. It had to be the casting directors!

"Do you mind if we just . . . ?" one of them, a man with a clipboard, asked Ms. Wells, indicating the fold-up chairs at the side of the room.

"Not at all, help yourself," Ms. Wells told them. "We'll carry straight on, if you don't mind."

"Please do," the other person, a woman with a shining blond bob said. She sat down and smiled at all of the girls, before taking a large notepad and pen from her bag.

Grace elbowed Ellie. "It's them!" she mouthed, her face anxious.

Ellie nodded, her own heart racing. It sure looked like it.

"When you're ready, Mrs. Edwards . . ." Ms. Wells said to the pianist. "And . . . off you go, Bryony."

Bryony's usually smiling face looked tense as she set off across the room. There was an unusual stillness in the room, as if everybody was holding their breath. *Poor Bryony*, thought Ellie sympathetically. It was bad enough having to dance the steps first before Ms. Wells's sharp eyes, but in front of the casting directors too was double the stress!

"And turn . . . and . . . use your tummy for the *pas de chat*!" Ms. Wells called. "Lovely. Remember to keep pulled up. Good girl. Who's next?"

One by one, the girls danced across the room. Ellie thought Grace was wonderful, even though she looked tense and strained. Lara was good, too. But Megan stumbled on the *temps levé*, the hop step, and turned bright red. And Sophie took off so high in her *pas de chat* that she landed awkwardly. The noise of her feet thumping down seemed to echo horribly around the room, and Ellie's heart skipped a beat. Now she was starting to wish *she* could have danced first. At least she would have gotten it over with quickly!

Ellie's palms felt clammy as she waited in line. The casting directors were scribbling notes about each girl who danced. She wished they could have come in earlier, to see her *sautés*, which had been so good! "Leap higher, and higher," Ms. Wells had urged them. "Think of it as a leap of faith—trust in yourself that you'll come down safely—and *push* yourself on!"

Ellie had loved the idea of a "leap of faith" across the ballet floor. *I trust in myself*, she'd thought, as she soared off the ground. *I can do it, I can do it!* And, to her delight, she had indeed managed to jump higher than ever before.

"And, Ellie—off you go," said Ms. Wells now, interrupting her thoughts.

Ellie tried to smile at the directors, but her face felt frozen. *Hey, calm down!* she ordered herself. *It's not make or break on this one sequence, okay?*

The pianist started and off Ellie went. *Pas de bourrée* first, the quick, running step Ellie usually loved. Yet today, her legs felt heavy and sluggish for some reason. *Come on, Ellie; keep it light*, she could hear Mrs. Franklin, her old teacher, reminding her in her head.

"And . . . fifth for *pas chassés*," Ms. Wells reminded. "Use the floor, Ellie, that's it."

Ellie liked the *chassé*—or "chased" step. They had practiced it endlessly the day before across the studio. And of course, yesterday, while each of Ellie's *balancés* had been neat and tight, today, she felt that she hadn't quite transferred her weight from foot to foot correctly, and . . .

She was fretting so much about messing up that before she knew it, she was at the far side of the room, and it was Kate's turn.

Ellie grimaced at Grace. She knew she hadn't danced her best. "You were fine," Grace assured her in a whisper. "*And* you were smiling!"

Ellie's eyebrows shot up. "*Was* I?" she asked. She'd been so tense she almost forgot to smile! *Well, that's something*, she thought in relief.

Grace nodded. "You were good," she whispered.

Ellie smiled gratefully at her friend. "Let's hope you're not the only one who thinks so." Her eyes slid over to the casting directors who were now watching Kate carefully. She really hoped they would stay for more of the lesson. She knew she could dance better than she just had. She really wanted to show them exactly what she was capable of!

To Ellie's relief, the casting directors did stay a while longer, and then called Ms. Wells over to ask her a few hushed questions, glancing over at the girls and looking over their notes. Then, a couple of days later, they were back, to watch the girls at the barre and practice *pirouettes* in the center. To make up for her nerves the previous time, Ellie did a perfect double *pirouette*—the first time she'd ever managed it!

As Ellie came to a stop, she saw the male casting director nodding approvingly—and the female director smiled and gave her a wink! "Very nice, Ellie," Ms. Wells said.

Ellie felt a warm glow that lasted the whole day, every time she thought about it. Sure, it was awful when you knew you'd danced a step badly. But boy, was it ever awesome when you knew you'd danced your best!

·　　·　　·　　·

The second weekend of term seemed very quiet. Lots of the other Year 7 girls had decided to go home for the weekend.

After waving Grace off at the front of the house, Ellie returned to the dorm feeling a little down. The week had been so busy in school, but now that the hectic routine had stopped, she found herself badly missing home and her old friends. There was a shopping trip planned to Sheen, the nearby high street, but first Ellie wanted to make a few calls in privacy. It wasn't often that the dorm was empty. She pulled out her cell phone and pressed the button for home. *Ring, ring, ring . . . click . . .*

"Hi," she heard her own voice say, "Ellie and Amy can't take your call right now. But if you leave us a message, we'll call you back real soon. Good-byeeee!"

Ellie bit her lip. It was like hearing a ghost, her own voice coming back down the line at her from the answering machine. Then she remembered. Of course! Mom and Steve had gone off hiking together this weekend, hadn't they? She hung up without leaving a message, then pressed Phoebe's home number.

"Ellie, what a nice surprise!" Diana Minton said. "Are you having a lovely time?"

"Yes, thanks," Ellie replied, trying to sound as enthusiastic as she usually felt about school. "Yeah, it's great, thanks. Um . . . is Pheebs around?"

"She's not, love, no. Sorry," Mrs. Minton said. "She was at a sleepover last night at Chloe's house, and a whole gang of them are going ice-skating later. You might catch her this evening, if you want to ring back then?"

"Okay," Ellie said, wondering who Chloe was. Somebody new at school, she guessed. And who was "the gang," anyway?

After she'd ended the call Ellie sighed, already feeling a bit left out of life in Oxford. *Come on, though, Ell*, she reasoned with herself. *Like you'd swap The Royal Ballet School for anything else in the world? I don't think so.*

She heard the door creak open, and footsteps.

"Are you coming, Ellie? The minibus is here!" Sophie called.

"Sure," Ellie replied, jumping to her feet. "I'll just grab my bag."

Downstairs, Bryony, Matt, and Kate were all clambering onto the minibus, along with some students from Year 8. Ellie and Sophie squeezed onto a seat together and off they went.

As the minibus pulled away from school, Ellie peered out of the window and spotted a figure sitting up in the old larch tree in the grounds. It looked familiar. She craned her neck to see who it was.

It was Lara. Ellie nudged Bryony. "What's Lara doing on her own up there?" she asked. "Why isn't she coming out with us?"

"It's her gran's birthday today—and the family have promised they'd call Lara this morning so her gran could have a nice long chat with her," Bryony explained. "Lara wants to be ready for the call, so as not to disappoint her gran."

They both caught a last glimpse of Lara in the tree as the bus went out of the school gates. Seeing her all alone in the tree, while the rest of them were all going off together, Ellie couldn't help feeling a bit sorry for her. But before she could think about it anymore, Sophie persuaded the bus driver to turn on the radio and began to sing along, and Ellie found herself laughing with the others at the silly words Sophie was making up.

·   ·   ·   ·

It was almost a culture shock, being in Sheen for the morning and being reminded that there was a whole world going on outside White Lodge. Ever since she'd started Lower School, Ellie's life had become ballet, ballet, ballet. It was odd to be on a normal street again, with ordinary people who weren't even slightly interested in *sautés* and *pliés*.

Ellie and the other Year 7s and 8s were chaperoned by some of the teachers, as they were the youngest students in the school.

"You can trust us," Sophie wheedled. "We won't get lost if you let us go on our own."

Mr. Whitehouse, their geography teacher, who'd been assigned to go with Ellie's group, laughed. "Sorry, kids," he said. "You have to wait until you're a great big grown-up Year 9-er for that."

The high street that ran through the small community of East Sheen was full of nice shops and cafes. Ellie and her friends went to a newsstand first and bought magazines, then went to a drugstore to try on nail polish and lip gloss, while the boys browsed in a CD store. Then they all hung out in a coffee shop for a while, drinking sodas and watching the world go by from the comfort of slippery leather sofas.

"I could fall asleep right here," Sophie said drowsily, leaning back. "What a week!"

Ellie took another sip of her raspberry milkshake. "It's only when you stop rushing around you realize how tired you are," she agreed. "Do you think anyone would mind if we all crashed for an afternoon nap?"

Matt made loud snoring noises, and everyone laughed.

It was fun to be out of school with her new friends, Ellie thought happily. She could hardly believe that she'd only known them a matter of days. Already it was difficult to imagine life without them!

Dear Diary,

It's Sunday night and I'm squeezed on the sofa in the common room with Sophie, Grace, and Bryony. Lara's gone off on her own again. She's been doing that all weekend—we've seen hardly anything of her. Not that I mind—at least it means that she doesn't get to snap at me! I bet she's sneaking in loads of extra practice. She never stops exercising her feet with the flexiband that the physio gave her.

It's nice to have a full dorm again—it does feel weird at night when half the beds are empty.

I was really pleased to see Grace when she got back tonight. Sounds like she had an awesome weekend. She's really good at keeping in touch with all her friends; it made me feel a bit guilty for not writing to Pheebs more often.

Anyway, better go—Sophie's starting a video right now!

Chapter 7

"I don't suppose anybody here is interested in hearing the cast list for *The Nutcracker*, are they?"

Ellie gulped at the sight of the paper Ms. Wells was holding. It was morning ballet class—and she had been kind of feeling sleepy. Now, suddenly she was wide awake!

"Yes!" Ellie and the others chorused at once.

Ms. Wells laughed. "Well, I won't keep you in suspense. Here goes—I'm very proud to tell you that five of you have been given parts. In Cast A, we have Kate as a doll, and Bryony and Ellie as party children. And Cast B, we have Lara as one of the party children, and Megan as a doll. Well done, all of you—and I'm sorry that not all of you could be picked this time. There will be other productions."

A buzz went around the room. Ellie felt giddy with excitement. *Wow!* She'd been picked to dance at The Royal Opera House, and as one of the party children too—just what she'd dreamed of!

Ms. Wells smiled at everyone then continued. "The production opens at The Royal Opera House on the 1st of December. Cast rotas and rehearsal times are up on the main school noticeboard, so please note down when you'll be needed. Basically, Cast A will dance at the opening performance, and then alternate with Cast B."

"I can't believe it!" she cried breathlessly to Grace—but one look at Grace's wretched face took the edge off her own happiness. Grace hadn't been picked! Ellie could hardly believe *that* either. What had the selectors been thinking, not to pick wonderful Grace?

"Oh, Grace," she said, hugging her friend. "They must have been crazy not to pick you."

Grace shrugged. "It's my own fault," she said, her face pale. "I was so nervous, dancing in front of the selectors, I know I didn't dance my best."

Ellie didn't know what to say, so she just squeezed Grace's hand sympathetically. Sophie, meanwhile, didn't seem so upset—she rushed over to hug Ellie and congratulate her.

Then Ellie caught Bryony's eye and they grinned at each other. Ellie felt bad for Grace, but she couldn't help her own excitement. Hey—she and Bryony were going to be party children together! What fun!

Lara, meanwhile, looked a bit grumpy. Ellie stared at her in disbelief—what could Lara possibly be in a mood about? Surely it wasn't about being in Cast B? She was still going to be dancing in *The Nutcracker* with The Royal Ballet for heaven's sake!

"Now, as well as dancing in your own cast, you're also going to be understudying the same role in the other cast," Ms. Wells went on over the chatter. "It makes sense that if someone from

Cast A is ill, their Cast B understudy can step in to fill the part."

So she and Lara were going to be each other's understudies! Ellie couldn't help smiling at Lara, who looked distinctly unamused. Ellie was too happy to care. In fact, it seemed pretty funny.

"Rehearsals start the week after half-term," Ms. Wells said. "We can go over any problems you have in class, so do tell me how you're getting on. After all," she said, "I don't want anybody saying afterwards, who *was* the teacher of that dreary little party child? Didn't she teach her *anything*?"

Ellie laughed. "We promise we won't be dreary," she said. "Just for you, Ms. Wells."

"Glad to hear it," Ms. Wells said cheerfully. "Right! Let's do some ballet."

.   .   .   .

Ellie could hardly wait to tell her mom the news when classes had ended. She groaned out loud when the phone line was engaged. Oh, no—if her mom was talking to Steve or Grandma, Ellie just knew she was going to be ages! Ellie just *had* to get the news out of her somehow—before she burst!

She rushed to the computer room. She would send a joint e-mail instead to her mom—and Grandma and Gramps, Heather and Libby in Chicago—and Phoebe and Bethany.

Her fingers flew across the keys as she tapped out her message, so keen to get the news out into the big wide world. She pressed the send key with an excited flourish—then, feeling ridiculously happy, she started back toward the dorm.

She had only been back in the dorm for a few minutes when her phone started ringing. She laughed as she saw the caller display—Home—and pressed the receiver.

There was a squeal from the other end of the line. "Honey, I can't *believe* it!"

"Hi, Mom," Ellie said happily. "I guess you got my e-mail, then!"

"Oh, Ellie!" her mom cried. It sounded as if she was almost in tears. "I'm so proud of you! I was on the phone to somebody from work, then as soon as I hung up, Grandma was on the line, telling me to check my e-mail. She said she and Gramps are going to arrange their vacation in England so they can come and see you dance in the opening performance. And Steve's parents are going to be back from Australia by then—so he thinks they'll want to come, too. Oh, honey, it's so exciting! I'm going to book us all tickets tomorrow!"

"Oh, wow!" Ellie cried, bursting with happiness at the thought of the people she loved most being there at her first performance on a professional stage. "That's so great! I can't wait!"

"Neither can I," said her mom. "I'm just the proudest mom that ever walked this Earth. Well done, Ellie!"

. . . .

The next couple of weeks passed quickly. Life was so *busy* at Lower School, what with classes and prep and everything else that Ellie was shocked when she realized it was the last weekend before half-term. Where had all the time gone? And how on earth would she fit in all *The Nutcracker* rehearsals for the rest of the term when her week was already stretched to bursting point?

Everyone seemed to be feeling the pressure, and most of Ellie's dorm had gone home for the weekend to recover and chill out. Ellie, Lara, Bryony, and Holly were the only Year 7 girls left at school. Bryony and Holly had gone to Sheen, promising to buy the others chocolate and facemasks for a girly night in. Ellie had taken advantage of the quiet to go back to bed for a morning nap. Bliss!

She woke up after an hour or so and stretched, enjoying the rarity of being able to lie around doing nothing. It was a fine, clear October morning, so Ellie grabbed a book, planning to find a warm, sheltered spot outside where she could curl up and read.

She pulled on her sneakers, and then went toward the Slip— only for her contented lazy feeling to disappear. For as she got nearer the Slip door, she could hear rippling piano music, and her heart sank. Lara was in there, playing the piano. The one person she *didn't* want to bump into.

Ellie stood listening for a few seconds. Often Lara played wild, whirling romps of music—she had taught them all "The Irish Rover" and "The Rose of Tralee." Today, however, she was playing something that sounded very mournful and slow. Ellie sighed. All she wanted to do was get outside and read her book. Would it be too rude of her to walk past Lara without saying a single word?

She hesitated. Yes, it *would* be rude, she reasoned, but then Lara was always rude to her. And frankly, she was sick of making all the effort. She took a deep breath, opened the door to the Slip, and started walking through, intending not to say anything.

Suddenly, though, the music stopped abruptly, and Ellie heard a sniff. She glanced warily over her shoulder, her hand on the door out to the corridor. To her great surprise, she saw that tears were rolling down Lara's face and plopping onto the piano keys.

Friend or no friend, Ellie couldn't ignore Lara now. "What's the matter?" she asked in astonishment. She could hardly believe what she was seeing—tough, independent Lara *crying*?

Lara jumped, as if she'd been unaware of Ellie's presence, then she fiercely rubbed her eyes, and spun around. The tears had left streaks down her pale face. "Nothing," she muttered, turning back to the piano and pounding out some loud chords.

Ellie hovered uncertainly. "Did something happen?" she asked.

"What's it to you?" Lara asked. It was the kind of rude brush-off Ellie was used to hearing from Lara, but she didn't sound quite as tough as usual today. In fact, there was a distinct catch in her voice.

Ellie shrugged. "Nothing," she said. "But I can listen, if you want to talk about it." There was a pause. "I mean, I know we haven't exactly gotten along very well . . ." she began.

"We might have done if you hadn't kept pushing me over!" Lara snapped.

Ellie's breath came out in an angry rush. "*Or* if you hadn't been so bad-tempered with me all the time!" she retorted hotly.

She turned to go. "I give up. Forget I even asked!" she cried. *Lara McCloud is just impossible!* she thought furiously to herself. *Totally impossible!*

"Ellie, wait!" Lara called.

There was something in Lara's tone—a pleading, almost—that made Ellie hesitate. She turned back to glare at her, arms folded. "What now? Going to have another go at me, are you?" she asked.

Lara shook her head. "No," she said, sounding subdued. There was a pause. "Ignore me," she went on. "I'm just . . . feeling down. And I took it out on you—again. Sorry."

"Why are you feeling down?" Ellie asked warily. "Or are you going to tell me it's none of my business?"

To her surprise, Lara just looked down at the piano keys, her shoulders slumped. "It's my mam and dad's wedding anniversary today," she said in a low voice. "That tune I was playing? It's called 'A Pair of Brown Eyes.' Daddy always plays it for her on their anniversary. I really wish . . ." She played another chord, this one more melancholic, and sniffed again.

"What?" Ellie prompted, the fierceness gone from her voice. She'd never heard Lara talk like this before.

Lara stared dully at the piano keys. "I wish I was there, with them and all my brothers and sisters," she said, all the fight gone from her voice. "I wish . . . Sometimes I wish I'd never come here."

Ellie's mouth fell open. That was the last thing she'd been

expecting to hear. *"What?"* she said. "Why? Don't you like being here?"

Lara wiped her eyes with her knuckles. "I just miss everybody back home so much," she said, with a sob in her voice. "I've never been away from them before. I just . . ." She pulled a tissue from her pocket and blew her nose. "Everyone else seems to have settled in fine. Everyone else seems so happy to be here. But I . . ." She shook her head, and then turned her head to meet Ellie's eyes at last. "I feel so, so homesick."

Ellie's mouth fell open in shock. She could hardly believe that Lara was saying such things—and to her, of all people! She struggled to find the right words. "You know, I do kind of understand," she said slowly. "When we moved to England from the U.S. last year, I missed my old life like crazy." She paused, trying to remember exactly how it had been. "Just little things, like going to see Gran and Gramps on the way home from school. All my friends. Even American candy."

Lara was quiet, listening. Ellie went on. "It took a while, but you know what? Now I'm glad we moved. I've met tons of great people. I'm here, at The Royal Ballet School, even!" She paused. "I guess I just realized that life can be good wherever you are. You know, now that I'm here, I miss my friends from Chicago *and* my friends from Oxford. But I've got Grace, and Sophie and Bryony and Matt . . . And I get to study ballet here every day! I guess there are good things and bad things wherever you are, right?"

Lara nodded, but her eyes were still miserable. She blew her nose again. "I can't help thinking that once I'm home, I won't want to come back here," she confessed. "You know everybody's so wild about *The Nutcracker*? Well, I'm not. Cos I don't even think I'll be here. I reckon I'll have left Lower School, gone back to high school in Ireland." She shuffled her feet under the piano. "You probably think I'm mad," she added.

"I don't," Ellie said staunchly. "There were times in Oxford when all I wanted to do was jump on a plane back to the U.S. and have my old life back." She looked at Lara. "But I stuck it out. It was hard, but it was worth it. Sometimes I guess you just have to . . ." She paused, trying to think of the right words. Then Ms. Wells's phrase came back to her from an earlier ballet lesson. "I guess you could say, you just have to take a 'leap of faith' that everything's going to work out okay." Ellie paused, then cleared her throat. "And we all know you're the best 'leaper' in ballet class."

Lara looked up and gave her a half-smile. "Ellie Brown, that is a terrible joke," she said. "You should be ashamed of yourself."

Ellie laughed. *I made Lara McCloud smile!* she thought to herself. It felt like a minor miracle. "You think that's bad?" she said. "I've got plenty worse than that." She touched Lara on the shoulder. "Seriously, though. It kills me to say this to you when you've been so mean to me, but . . . well, you're such an awesome dancer, you can't leave now. Give The Royal Ballet School a bit longer."

Lara picked out the tune she'd been playing earlier with a

single finger. "I don't know, Ellie," she said, looking weary. "I just don't know if I can."

Ellie stood up, feeling a little awkward. She didn't quite know what else to say. Then Lara started to play another tune, and Ellie took that as her cue to leave. She'd tried her best. She'd been nice to Lara, hadn't she? Tried to help her. And for once—just for a few minutes—Lara had been sort of nice back.

It was an improvement, anyway—wasn't it?

Dear Diary,

I was so shocked to find out that Lara has been homesick all along. That must be why she's been sending so many e-mails and letters to her friends—because she misses them so desperately. Talk about pride. I'd never have guessed she felt like that. I hope that I convinced her to give things a chance here. It would be awful if she left school because she was too homesick to carry on here.

The thing about Lara is it's so hard to know what she's thinking. She's so headstrong; who knows whether she'll listen to me. But here's hoping . . .

We had a fun girly night tonight. Green

mud face packs, sparkly nail polish, candy bars, and gossip all around! Lara didn't even say anything mean to me! But I wouldn't go so far as to say that she likes me!

Signing off quickly—Mrs. Hall's footsteps approaching!

The weeks leading up to half-term felt almost as momentous as the week before Christmas. Everyone was so excited, counting down the days, hours, and lessons until they were due to go home. Grace had already packed most of her things to take home by Monday night. And Sophie seemed to spend the entire last week in school texting and calling friends, arranging endless things to do in the weeklong mid-semester break.

"Sophie, I hope you'll have time to fit in some ballet practice, what with all of these social engagements," Ellie said, in her best Ms. Wells voice, wagging a stern finger.

Sophie widened her eyes. "Who, me? I'll be working my body to exhaustion every single day, of course," she joked. "I mean—you've seen my devotion to practice, girls. You know how dedicated I am!"

Bryony fished out the flexiband that was gathering dust under Sophie's bed. "So you'll be wanting to pack this then, won't you, oh dedicated one?" she teased.

Sophie looked slightly sheepish. "I suppose I'd better," she said. "There's a first time for everything!"

By Friday night, nobody could talk about anything but half-term and what they were going to do and eat, and who they were going to hang out with. *The Nutcracker*, school gossip, ballet . . . all were forgotten for once. Lara was the sunniest Ellie had ever seen her, talking nonstop about her beloved family back home and how much she was dying to see them.

"Oh, I hope my wee brother's at the airport to meet me," she kept saying to anyone who was listening. "Darling Danny, he's such a sweetie. Look at this photo and just tell me he's not the most gorgeous wee thing!"

Ellie felt pleased that Lara was so happy, but she couldn't help wondering if they would see her again, come the start of term. She hadn't told anybody about their conversation in the Slip, and Lara hadn't referred to it again. It was almost as if it had never happened. But at least Lara wasn't being rude to Ellie anymore.

. . . . .

On Saturday morning, the girls' dorm was a whirlwind of excitement. Some of the students could hardly eat their breakfast. The boys and girls were waiting in their dorms until their parents arrived.

"I'm guessing Grace's mum will arrive first—if she's as super-punctual as our little Virgoan Grace," Sophie said.

Grace grinned back. "I reckon your mum will be last then, Soph—too busy gossiping with the neighbors if she's anything like you!" She laughed as Sophie's mouth fell open in mock outrage. "In fact, girls, does anyone want to make a bet that

Sophie's folks just won't turn up at all? They must be loving the peace and quiet without her."

Sophie started to reply, but someone interrupted her with an excited squeal. "Megan! Isn't that your dad down there?"

The other girls rushed to the window to watch a tall, sandy-haired man getting out of a minivan. "Dad!" screamed Megan immediately, waving like a lunatic from the window.

"Wrong, then, Sophie!" grinned Grace, as Megan ran around saying breathless good-byes and hugging everybody.

After Megan had grabbed her bags and left, there was a moment's silence. And then everybody ran back to the windows to see who was going to be next.

Grace's mom did arrive soon afterward, closely followed by Sophie's parents, to laughs all around. Then Mrs. Hall put her head around the door. "Lara? The minibus will take you to Heathrow airport for your flight home in five minutes, okay?"

Lara's pale face turned bright red, and all her freckles vanished for a moment. "I'm on my way," she said, her eyes sparkling. She hugged Bryony and some of the other girls, and then came over to Ellie. "I never said thank you for the other night," she said in a low voice. "You were nice to me when I've been so . . ."

Ellie felt a little awkward, and tried to turn it into a joke. "So horrible? So rude?" she suggested sweetly.

Lara grinned. "I deserve that," she said. "I've been such an auld misery toward you. I don't know how it got so out of hand really. Except that, we got off to a bad start—and then I was feeling down, so I snapped at you some more—and then . . . it was hard to suddenly change and start being nice to you. Pride, I suppose . . ." she finished sheepishly. Tentatively, she stuck out a hand. "I'm truly sorry, Ellie."

Ellie took Lara's hand in her own and smiled. "Have a good vacation, Lara. And . . . have you thought any more about what we talked about?"

"I'm still not sure," Lara said with a sigh. "What did you call it? A leap of faith?" She picked up her bags and shook her head. "I just don't know if I can do that," she said quietly. "But thanks for trying." Then she raised her voice and smiled around the room. "Have a good week, everybody."

"You too," Ellie said. "See you next Sunday." She tried not to make it sound like too much of a question.

Lara didn't reply. Ellie bit her lip as she skipped out of the room, and wondered if she'd ever see her skipping back in again. But before she could dwell on it, Bryony was calling, "Ellie. Hey, Ellie! Isn't that your mum down there?"

It was. It was! Her mom and Steve were gazing up at the building, searching for her face. She let out a whoop of joy. "See you later, girls! Good-bye!"

●　　　●　　　●　　　●

It had been just six weeks since Ellie had been in Oxford, but it felt like a lot longer when Amy finally pulled up outside their apartment building. It was the strangest sensation—being somewhere so familiar that suddenly felt so *unfamiliar*. Already, Ellie had been wondering what her friends from Lower School were all doing. Lara would be on the plane by now, she guessed, maybe even about to land at Dublin airport. Grace's mom had a special lunch planned to celebrate Grace being home. And Sophie would be helping out at her little brother's birthday party—"the chimps' tea party" she'd called it. No doubt she'd be wearing a silly hat and handing out cupcakes right now.

Ellie, on the other hand, didn't have an awful lot planned. Phoebe's family was spending a few days with Phoebe's grandmother in Cornwall, a county in the southwest corner of Britain. Pheebs had pushed a note under the Browns' door before she'd left:

> *Ellie! You're back! Can't wait to see you. If you're around on Wednesday, it would be great to meet up and go into town together. You can meet some of the other girls from school—I think you'll really like them—and of course, they're dying to meet you!*

Ellie liked the sound of that. She was looking forward to catching up with Phoebe again. In the meantime, she spent most of the weekend hanging out with her mom and Steve in Oxford. They went out for lunch in a beautiful old restaurant by the river Thames, and then Ellie and her mom did some shopping in town together, while Steve went to see his beloved football team, Oxford United, play a home match.

On Sunday, it poured with rain, so the three of them went to see a movie in the afternoon. The rain had stopped by the time the movie finished, so they bought fish-and-chips, Ellie's favorite English food, and walked home, eating the hot, salty chips as they went.

Ellie's friend Bethany came over on Monday. Ellie had met Bethany at the local ballet school, and they'd gone to JAs together. Bethany had been desperate to get a place at The Royal Ballet School herself but had missed out after the Final Audition, unfortunately. Despite her own disappointment, Bethany was almost as excited as Ellie was when she heard that Ellie had been accepted. Ellie really admired Bethany. She wasn't sure that she could have been quite so supportive and interested, if things had been the other way around.

"Tell me *all* about it," Bethany demanded, as soon as the two of them were in Ellie's bedroom. "Everything! Your e-mails have been brilliant, but it's not the same as talking about The Royal Ballet School. And what have you been learning in ballet class there?"

"It is so hard," Ellie confessed to Bethany. "It's not like Mrs. Franklin's class where we were her star pupils—*everybody* is amazing at The Royal Ballet School. I am totally, totally average there, which is kind of hard to get used to."

"Scary," agreed Bethany. "What's your teacher like?"

"Ms. Wells? She's nice—but strict. And she spots absolutely everything!" Ellie said. "Even if your little finger is slightly in the wrong position—she's over there, correcting it. Honestly, she's like a hawk. But it's good, too. You can't get away with anything—I feel like I've learned so much, just in a few weeks."

"Wow!" said Bethany. "Oh, Ell, it all sounds so fab!"

"It is," Ellie said. "It so, so is." She was standing in an *arabesque*, holding on to the windowsill. "We're going on pointe in January. I am so excited. I guess I told you that in an e-mail, right?"

Bethany nodded. "And I can't wait to see your opening night at The Royal Opera House," she said. "I hope we get seats near the front!" She grinned. "You are *so* lucky, Ellie Brown," she said. "D'you know that? So, so lucky."

"I know," Ellie said solemnly. Did she ever know! She told herself the same thing every single day she woke up at school. But the thought was still nagging at her—had *Lara* realized how lucky she was to be studying at The Royal Ballet School? Oh, she really hoped Lara had a good friend like Bethany to make her see that!

•　　　•　　　•　　　•

On Wednesday, Phoebe's family got back from their trip to Cornwall, and Ellie couldn't hide her delight to see her friend. She had really missed her over the last few weeks. Letters and phone calls just weren't the same as having funny, friendly Phoebe right there in person!

"We got back really late last night—I wanted to knock on your front door in case you and your mum were still up, but . . ." Phoebe grinned ruefully, "Mum went bananas when I mentioned it. Said *absolutely not, Phoebe Minton!* So I had to wait until this morning. Anyway—did you get my note? Do you fancy going into town today?"

"Sure," Ellie smiled. She'd been so looking forward to spending time with Pheebs again, she'd been dressed and ready to go since eight-thirty that morning. "When are we going?"

Phoebe glanced at her watch. "Ten minutes? I'll just phone a couple of the others, check they're still around. I'll be back over as soon as I can!"

Phoebe was as good as her word. Exactly ten minutes later, she and Ellie were running down the apartment steps together, heading for town. Phoebe had arranged to meet her other friends in the Clarendon Center, a modern shopping mall in central Oxford.

Phoebe and Ellie hopped on a bus, chattering nonstop. Ellie had almost forgotten how much her friend liked to talk! "You'll really like Chloe, she's fab. And Leah's really funny, too. And Molly is just the prettiest girl in school, you'd be able to tell as soon as you meet her . . ."

Once they'd all met up and Ellie had been introduced to Chloe, Leah, Molly, Tess, Sujinder, and two other girls whose names she couldn't remember, Phoebe suggested they go for a smoothie so they could catch up on everybody's news.

"You have missed sooo much, Pheebs," Chloe said, rolling her eyes dramatically as they sat down in a nearby cafe together. "Are you going to tell her, Leah, or shall I?"

Dark-haired Leah blushed. "I went ice-skating with Joshua on Saturday afternoon," she told them.

"WHAT?!" Phoebe screeched, jumping up and nearly knocking the table flying. "No way! Is this a wind-up?"

Leah shook her head. "No. We went ice-skating together and then . . ."

"What? What? Are you two *going out* now? Did you *kiss* him?" Phoebe could barely get the words out fast enough. She turned to Ellie hurriedly. "Joshua's in our class, and we could tell he fancied Leah, but she's always denied it—and now . . ."

Leah sipped her milkshake daintily. "I'm meeting up with him later this afternoon," she said, skirting the kiss question.

"Wow," Phoebe said. "I leave Oxford for five minutes and this happens! What else?"

Ellie was starting to feel a little left out, as the conversation went from Leah and Joshua to Molly's new baby niece to whether Chloe could get away with wearing her new black boots to school as part of uniform, to how dreamy the new student teacher Mr. Andrews was . . .

"Sorry, Ell," Phoebe said after a few minutes, "this must be really boring for you. Tell us about being at The Royal Ballet School."

"What are the boys like? Is it true they wear tutus?" Chloe

wanted to know between giggles.

Ellie smiled. "No—but they do wear leotards and tights," she said.

"Can you imagine some of the boys in our class in leotards and tights?" Molly squealed. "What about Paul Gibson? Ugh!"

"With his long skinny legs!" Sujinder added, choking with mirth.

Ellie smiled, but inside she felt a pang of homesickness for her own Year 7, where nobody thought twice about boys in leotards and tights. In fact, nobody thought much about the boys at all, other than as friends. Phoebe's new friends seemed to treat them like a different species.

Chloe drained her drink and got to her feet. "Right—who's up for some shopping?" she asked. "Mum's given me some money for a new top so I thought I'd get something for Mia's party on Saturday. What are you guys wearing?"

As everybody chattered happily about which outfits they were considering, Ellie leaned over to Phoebe. "Pheebs, I'm sorry, but I'm going to have to go," she said. It was a small fib, but she was feeling so left out of Phoebe's new gang that she just wanted to go home. She hadn't a clue who all these people were that they kept talking about, and it was making her feel as if she was really quiet and boring, sitting there, unable to join in the conversation.

"Already?" Phoebe said. "But we've only just got here!"

"I know," Ellie said, "but I promised Mom I'd . . . um . . . help with lunch."

It sounded lame, even to Ellie, but Phoebe just nodded. "If

you're sure . . . ?" she asked. "Can we catch up later in the week, maybe?"

"Yeah," Ellie said. "That would be nice. See you soon." She cleared her throat. "Nice to meet you, everyone," she said, smiling as brightly as she could. "I've got to go."

Ellie strode back through the shopping center toward the bus stop. *Everything's changed*, she thought glumly. *In six weeks, everything's changed.*

⋅   ⋅   ⋅   ⋅

Ellie was in a funny mood when she got back to the apartment. But she wasn't the only one—her mom was acting kind of weird, too.

"Smoked salmon bagels for lunch?" Ellie marveled, sitting down at the table. She and her mom usually only had smoked salmon as a treat at Christmas. "Did you win the lottery while I was out, or something?"

Her mom had a strange smile on her face. "Kind of . . ." she said. "What would you like to drink?"

"Um . . . milk, I guess," Ellie replied, staring at her mom. "What's going on?" she asked suspiciously.

Her mom poured them both a glass of milk each and sat down opposite her. "Ellie," she began slowly, "something fantastic has happened." Then she paused. "At least, I think it's fantastic. I so hope that *you* think it's fantastic, too, otherwise . . . well, otherwise I'll have to have a re-think. Because I want you to be really honest about how you feel about it, and—"

"What?" Ellie cried impatiently. "What on earth has happened?" Had her mom *really* won the lottery? Or had she been offered a new job? Or . . .

"Steve's asked me to marry him," her mom said.

Ellie's jaw swung open. "Marry him?" Ellie repeated. She stared at her mom, feeling stunned.

Ellie's mom's eyes turned anxious. "I guess it is kind of sudden," she said.

Ellie swallowed hard, trying to take in the news. She was also trying to figure out exactly how she felt. It was good to see her mom so happy and in love, of course, but . . . married? "When did this happen?" she managed to croak.

"This morning," her mom replied. "He dropped the mail off earlier—and this, too." She fished a beautiful diamond ring from out of her pocket to show Ellie, then smiled at the memory. "He got down on one knee, and everything. Honestly, it was ridiculous, Ellie. I just had fits of giggles—I thought he was messing around but . . ." She smiled, and her eyes were soft. "He meant it."

"Wow," Ellie gulped. "So . . . what did you say?"

Ellie's mom suddenly looked nervous all over again. "I wanted to talk to you first," she said. "Because it's really important to both of us what you think about all of this. If you're not comfortable with it, things can stay exactly as they are."

There was a pause.

Then Ellie threw her arms around her mom's neck. "Of course I'm pleased!" she cried. "Steve is great. Congratulations!

Get on the phone to him at once, and tell him you'll marry him!" She meant it, too. Steve made her mom really happy—happier than she'd ever seen her before. Sure, it was going to be strange, becoming a family of three when it had been just Ellie and her mom for as long as she could remember, but she'd get used to it.

Ellie's mom let out a huge sigh of relief. "I'm so glad, honey," she said, squeezing Ellie tightly. "I love him so much. I never thought I'd be able to say that again, after your dad died. But I can. I do. He makes me feel really . . . wonderful. I'll call him right now!"

As her mom settled in the armchair with the phone, Ellie found herself wanting to tell Phoebe the news, too. She popped out of the front door—only to see Phoebe coming out her front door at the same time!

"Guess what, Pheebs?" Ellie cried, and she told her all about it.

"Wow! They don't mess about, do they?" Phoebe said, when Ellie had finished. "That's so exciting!"

"I know, isn't it? Mom's on the phone right now, telling him yes, she'll marry him," Ellie said. Then she stopped. "Were you coming over to see me?"

Phoebe looked down at her feet. "I was," she admitted. "I felt a bit bad about this morning in town. I know you were feeling left out and I didn't do much to help. So I came to say sorry."

Ellie hugged her, her earlier glum feelings totally gone. "No worries," she said easily. "Want to come in?"

"Sure," Phoebe said, following Ellie back to the Browns' apartment. She was spinning her bangle watch around on her wrist. "I guess I didn't want to ask too much about *your* new life because I was worried you'd tell me how much more glamorous and exciting than me your new friends are," she confessed.

Ellie snorted as they went through to the kitchen. "And there I was, feeling really boring compared to *your* new friends!" she said. "We're as bad as each other, aren't we?"

Phoebe grinned. "Here's to being boring," she joked. "So anyway. You can tell me all about The Royal Ballet School now—and I promise I won't be jealous."

Ellie grinned back. "It's a deal," she said.

Dear Diary,

I'm all packed up ready for school again tomorrow—and I'm looking forward to going. Dying to catch up with the others and get back to ballet!

The last few days of break have been fun. Phoebe and I went roller-skating together and laughed ourselves silly, and I went to see Mrs. Franklin with Bethany, and that was really nice. Plus Mom has been buying piles of wedding magazines that we've been giggling over. I'm going to be Maid of Honor, but she's promised I don't have to wear anything too frilly or icky!

We're having a girls' night in tonight. There's a good movie on TV and I just happened to see a new tub of double chocolate ice cream in the freezer . . .

Chapter 9

"Hi, guys," Ellie smiled, walking back into the dorm. It really felt like coming home—her second home, if that was possible. She glanced around. Grace was back, sorting out all her clothes, and there was Sophie doing a headstand on her bed, with Bryony waving from the corner. The only person missing was . . .

"Um . . . where's Lara?" Ellie asked. She felt oddly disappointed. Was Lara not coming back to school, after all? Even though they'd had their differences, Ellie knew the dorm wouldn't be the same without Lara.

"She's not back yet," Grace replied, coming over to hug Ellie. "So how was your week? Any gossip?"

"*Major* gossip!" Ellie announced, with a grin. "My mom's getting married!"

The others squealed with excitement, wanting to hear all about it. Yet as Ellie told them, she felt distracted. Her eyes kept flicking across to the door, wondering if Lara was going to make an appearance. *Come on, Lara,* she thought in her head, *make the leap!*

Just as Ellie had decided that Lara had chosen to stay in

Ireland, the door opened, and in she came.

"You're here!" Ellie cried.

Lara gave her a smile. "I'm here," she echoed.

Sophie was giving them both odd looks. "Since when did you two get to be buddies?" she wanted to know.

"Oh, it's a long story," Lara said airily, with a wink at Ellie.

"All that bickering and fighting . . . it's water under the bridge now," Ellie joked. "Right, Lara?"

"Bickering? Fighting? Us?" Lara replied. "I can't even *remember* any bickering." She heaved her bags onto her bed. "Whew, it's good to be back with you guys. You know, after missing them like crazy for weeks on end, I spent the whole of half-term arguing with my brothers and sisters—especially the sister I used to share a bedroom with."

"No way!" Bryony cried. "What about?"

Lara smiled ruefully. "She'd gotten too used to having the room to herself. Oh boy, did she get her knickers in a twist at having to share again!" She shook her head. "Mad, isn't it? We nearly came to blows!" She pulled a couple of leotards out of her bag and held them a second before hanging them up. "So I'm back. And you know what that means?"

Ellie looked over. "Nope."

Lara raised an eyebrow. "Me, you, and Bryony, *Nutcracker* party children! Rehearsals start next Friday, don't they?"

Ellie grinned. "I'll try not to push you over," she joked, and then held her breath once the words were out. Lara *would* realize that was a joke, wouldn't she?

To her relief, Lara burst out laughing. "Sure you won't," she said.

"You're right, I won't," Ellie said, laughing too. "I wouldn't dare!"

.   .   .   .

Term started—and so did the rehearsals. It was going to mean a grueling countdown to Christmas, Ellie quickly realized. As one of the party children, Ellie was only in the first act of the show, but even so, she still seemed to be marked down for evening rehearsals two or three times a week.

As well as Ellie, Lara, and Bryony, some of the boys from their year had been picked to play party children too—Matt, Justin, and Oliver. There were also some students from Years 8 and 9—including Jessica, Ellie's guide.

"Ellie, congratulations!" she cried, grabbing Ellie's hands and swinging her around at the first rehearsal that Friday evening. "You've done really well, you know, being selected in your very first year here!"

"Your phone was ringing," Grace told Ellie as she came into the dorm afterward. "It went to voicemail—sorry, I didn't get there in time."

"Thanks," Ellie said, picking up her phone. She grinned as she heard her mom's excited voice on the voicemail.

"Hi, honey, it's Mom," the message began. "Guess what— we've booked the wedding! We've found this gorgeous place by the river and they had a last-minute cancellation for the 1st of December—so we've taken it!"

Ellie gaped. Was she hearing things? The 1st was her opening night at *The Nutcracker*!

"I know it's soon," her mom went on, "but we thought, with Grandma and Gramps being in England then, and Steve's parents back from Australia, we could tie in everything together, so everyone can come. Oh, and I think I found the perfect dress for me, and one for you, too. I'm going to send you a swatch of the fabric tomorrow."

The words were pouring out of the phone, but Ellie couldn't take them in.

"What else?" her mom finished up. "Oh, just to let you know, I've booked our tickets for the 12th, your opening night. There are eleven of us altogether—me and Steve, Grandma and Gramps, Steve's parents, Bethany and her mom, and the Mintons. It's going to be quite a party! I'd better go anyway—speak to you soon. Love you. Bye!"

Ellie jabbed the phone off, feeling stunned. Tickets for the 12th? What was her mom talking about? She wasn't even *dancing* on the 12th! And as for her mom booking the wedding on the 1st—*what* was happening?

"Everything all right?" Grace asked, sitting up on her bed and looking at Ellie curiously.

"No," Ellie said in a small voice. "Things aren't right at all." And she rushed blindly out of the room, not really knowing where she was going. There had been a big mistake somewhere along the line. Some huge communication breakdown! For some reason, her mom thought her opening night in *The Nutcracker* was the 12th! But why would she think that, when Ellie had told her it was the 1st?

Ellie tried to think rationally as she raced through the Slip, down the stairs, and outside. She stood in front of the school, gulping in the cool fall air. Actually, she remembered suddenly, she hadn't exactly *told* her mom the opening night was the 1st. She'd put it in the e-mail, hadn't she? She'd dashed off that e-mail to everybody, telling them the news about *The Nutcracker*. Surely she hadn't . . .

Ellie felt sick with panic. Surely she hadn't *typed in the wrong date*?

Ellie gulped in horror and raced to the computer room. With trembling fingers, she logged on and checked through her old e-mails. *Please let me have put the right date!* she thought frantically. *Please let me not have made a mistake!*

Okay, here it was, the e-mail she'd sent in such excitement. Her eyes scanned through it quickly.

> Dear guys,
>   Guess what? I've got the most awesome, awesome news for you all! I got a part in *The Nutcracker*! I'm going to be dancing on stage at The Royal Opera House with The Royal Ballet!

Seriously!!

I can't believe it either.

I am sooooo excited! AND I'm going to be dancing on the opening night—the 12 December!

Ellie put her head in her hands, then peeped through her fingers and slowly read the last sentence again.

AND I'm going to be dancing on the opening night—the 12 December!

Oh, no! Oh, *no*! She'd only gone and told everybody the wrong date! Her finger must have slipped—she must have pressed the one and two keys together, instead of pressing just one.

Ellie groaned. Whatever was she going to do now? Not only had her mom booked her wedding for the first night of *The Nutcracker*—but eleven people had spent tons of money on tickets to see her dance—when she wasn't even going to be on stage that night!

Dear Diary,

I am so, so stupid! I have messed everything up! What am I going to do? I feel like the biggest fool in the world. I can't believe I sent that e-mail with the wrong date—I will never, ever send another e-mail without checking every single thing in it*!!*

What am I going to do?

What am I going to DO???

I can't miss Mom's wedding. Even though I'll be gutted to give up dancing on the opening night, my only hope is that The Royal Ballet will allow me to swap that performance with someone—maybe Lara! So she'd have to agree too.

But Lara's not even here—she's gone to stay with an aunt in London this weekend. I'm going to have to wait until Sunday teatime before I can ask if she'd be willing to dance on the 1st for me.

And even if Lara says yes, I've got to tell Rose and Michael, the casting directors what a mess I've made of everything.

And then, even if they're cool with Lara and me swapping a performance, I've got to break it to Mom that she and everyone else has spent a fortune on the wrong tickets!

What a humongous mess!

Chapter 10

"Lara, can I have a word? I need a big, big favor. Massive, in fact. Huge."

Ellie had all but pounced upon Lara the moment she'd got back to school, late Sunday afternoon.

"Sure," Lara said easily, then frowned at Ellie's anxious face. "Ellie, what's the matter? Are you okay?"

"No," Ellie groaned. "I am seriously not okay. I really need your help."

She told Lara what had happened, and Lara whistled sympathetically. "What a nightmare!" she said.

"Exactly," Ellie said. "So I was wondering, is there any chance we can swap our first two nights? Would you dance the first for me, if I do the 2nd for you? That's if Rose lets us, of course."

Lara's green eyes sparkled. "Are you serious? Will I dance the opening night of the show for you?" She whooped in delight. "Of course I will! Swap your Saturday night for my Sunday matinee? Absolutely right I will!"

Ellie felt faint with relief. Well, that was the first hurdle cleared anyway. Now she just had to face the casting directors and break it to *them* that she'd gotten into a pickle. And that prospect was far worse! Rose and Michael were always telling the cast how dedicated they had to be if they ever hoped to make a career as dancers. Weren't they forever saying that the show had to come first?

Lara squeezed her hand when Ellie poured out her woes. "We'll go and see them together tomorrow," she said.

Ellie sighed. Another whole night to wait! She could hardly bear it!

.   .   .   .

After ballet class the next morning, Ellie and Lara ran straight to the Lower School Ballet Principal's office to try to get a telephone number for Rose, the casting director. By a stroke of luck, Rose was actually at the principal's desk, frowning at a sheaf of paperwork. "Hello there," she said, smiling as Ellie and Lara came tumbling in, red-faced and out of breath. "Are you looking for Mr. Knott? He's—"

"No," Ellie panted. "We were looking for you."

Rose peered closely at them. "Sit down, both of you. Is everything all right?"

"Not really, no," Ellie confessed. "My mom's wedding is on the opening night of the show—when I'm supposed to be dancing!"

Rose put her pen down. "Ahh," she said.

"I'm really sorry," Ellie went on, feeling wretched. "*Really* sorry. I promise I'll dance every other night you want me to, and I know the show has to come first, but I just can't miss the wedding, and . . ."

Rose looked appalled at the thought. "Of course you can't!" she said. "I wouldn't dream of asking you to miss your own mum's wedding."

Ellie's mouth shut with a snap. "You wouldn't?" she echoed.

"Absolutely not!" Rose said. "I'm a casting director, not some kind of monster!" She laughed at the relieved expression on Ellie's face. "Don't worry, we'll get one of the understudies to cover you. That's what they're there for!"

Ellie felt a load had been lifted off her shoulders. "So . . . so you don't mind?" she asked. Her mouth felt so dry, the words came out in a croak.

"Not at all," Rose said warmly. She pulled out a crumpled cast list from her bag. "Let's see . . ." she mused, running her finger along the names. Then she looked up at Lara. "Ah! I think I know now why you're here to see me too, Lara!"

Lara smiled.

"We were wondering if we could maybe do a swap," Ellie explained tentatively. "So that Lara dances on the 1st and I dance on the 2nd?"

The casting director nodded. "I don't see why not," she said. "If that's all right with you, Lara?"

Lara nodded. "I'd love to dance on the 1st!" she beamed.

Rose smiled at both of them. "Great. Then that's settled. I'll just make a note of it here . . . Okay." She looked up at them both. "And thanks for all the hard work you've been putting in at rehearsals, too—both of you. We were right to pick you both for the show."

Ellie smiled, feeling much better.

"Rose, Ellie has a problem with tickets, too," Lara blurted out. "Her family and friends have bought tickets for the performance on the 12th of December . . . by mistake . . . and now they'll need some for the 2nd. I don't suppose you know if there's anyone who might help her out, do you?"

Ellie shot Lara a look. She hadn't planned on telling Rose anything about the tickets!

Rose chuckled. "Oh dear, poor Ellie," she said. "What a weekend you've had. I can phone my friend Alison at The Royal Opera House box office, if you'd like? She might be able to switch your tickets around for you."

"Yes, please!" Ellie said eagerly, crossing her fingers. "I'll need eleven tickets for the 2nd, if there are any left."

Rose was already dialing. "Leave it with me," she said. "Is that Alison? Hi, Ali, it's Rose. Yeah, great thanks. Listen . . . small favor. Could you check to see if *The Nutcracker* has sold out on the 2nd December?"

Ellie could hardly bear to listen to the conversation.

Lara grabbed her hand and squeezed it tightly while they waited for Alison's reply.

Suddenly Rose was giving them the thumbs up. "There are? Could you wangle eleven seats together, please? Eleven good seats, if possible." She winked at Ellie. "And you'll be able to buy some tickets back for the 12th, too? Excellent."

As Rose put down the phone, Ellie felt like crying with sheer relief.

"All done," Rose said cheerfully. She patted Ellie's arm comfortingly over the desk. "And they're good seats, too."

It was all Ellie could do to stop herself from flinging herself at Rose and hugging her. "Thank you," she whispered. "I think you just saved my life."

• • • • •

Once Ellie had recovered from the trauma caused by one single typo—and her mom had confirmed that yes, everybody could still come to the ballet on the 2nd, and ooh, they *were* very good seats, much better than the ones they'd had for the 12th, the rest of November seemed to fly by.

"Only three weeks to go!" Ellie and her friends kept telling each other. "Only two weeks to go!" Then, "Only one more week!"

Ellie and the other party children had their costumes fitted, which made the whole thing seem even more real and exciting. Ellie's dress was scarlet with silver trim, and she had scarlet ribbons to wear in her hair, too. Bryony was in pale blue, and Lara was in green. Matt and the other boys were in beaded vests and funny little knickerbocker pants that ended at their knees, about which there was much embarrassed guffawing.

In the final week before the show, they had a dress rehearsal with full costume and makeup at The Royal Opera House. The stage seemed scarily enormous, and Ellie couldn't believe how different it felt to dance on stage, rather than in a studio, where she felt contained by the walls and the ceilings. Every time she took a step on the stage, she was aware of just how massive the auditorium was—and just how many people were going to be watching her!

"Next time we're here, it'll be for the real thing," Bryony said afterward, and Ellie felt a delicious thrill run down her spine. It seemed almost too exciting—and scary—to be true.

.   .   .   .

The day of the wedding dawned bright and frosty.

"A perfect winter's day," Ellie's mom said happily, looking out of the window. "Oh, Ellie, I'm so excited! I'm getting married!" She blew her nose.

Ellie put her arm around her. "Mom—I hope you're not crying under that tissue," she said mock severely.

"Just a bit—but only with happiness," her mom replied tearfully. "Oh, Ellie, I can hardly believe it."

Ellie's grandma came in the room just then, and laughed at her daughter's girlish expression. "Amy Brown, you'd better get a wriggle on," Ellie's gran said. "Beautiful as I think you look in your flannel pajamas, I'm sure your guests would rather see you dressed."

Ellie giggled as her mom looked at the time, gave a squeak, and dashed into the shower. "It is so nice having you and Gramps here," Ellie said, winding her fingers around her gran's neck like she used to when she was a little girl. "This is the best Christmas present of all."

Her gran kissed her on the top of her head. "We wouldn't have missed this day for the world," she said.

And neither would I, Ellie thought, a few hours later as she went into the register office behind her mom, who looked fantastic in a simple ivory dress, with a bunch of white roses. As the first chords of "Here Comes the Bride" were struck, London, and The Royal Opera House suddenly seemed a world away.

·   ·   ·   ·

"I now pronounce you . . . man and wife. You may kiss the bride."

As Steve bent forward to kiss her mom, Ellie leaned against her gramps. Just for a second, she felt sad that her mom was no longer all hers. But then, as she saw the smile on her mom's face, she pushed the thought away quickly. Her mom looked so happy. That was what counted today.

Grandma was blowing her nose, moist-eyed, on the other side of her, and reached across to squeeze Ellie's hand. "Doesn't she look lovely?" she whispered, her voice shaking with pride.

Ellie squeezed back. "She sure does," she replied.

Gramps winked at her. "Almost as lovely as our granddaughter," he said. "We're so proud of both of you."

"Aww, Gramps," Ellie said, blushing. She snuggled a little closer into her grandfather's side, smoothing down her rose-pink bridesmaid dress. She and Mom had both loved it, with its floaty full skirts and tiny embroidered roses on the corset. The hairdresser who'd come over that morning to do Amy's hair had woven rosebuds into both of their hairstyles, and Ellie felt like a princess.

Amy and Steve signed the registry and walked back down the aisle, out of the room. Ellie's grandma and gramps went over to speak to Steve's parents. Ellie found herself wondering, just for a moment, about *The Nutcracker*. Cast A—plus Lara—were due to be having a last rehearsal right now, and the matinee performance was due to start at two-thirty, less than two hours away . . .

"Ellie! Are you still on the planet?"

Ellie whipped her head around and smiled at Phoebe, who had danced up to her in a red shift dress and black patent leather shoes. "Hi, Pheebs," she said. "Wow, I don't think I've ever seen you in a dress before." She caught sight of Bethany across the room, too, looking gorgeous in a lilac dress.

Phoebe laughed. "You can talk—I'm not the one in the bridesmaid outfit!" she said. "I was all for wearing jeans, but Mum put her foot down." She twirled around. "Hey, Ell, are you going to teach me some funky dance moves on the dance floor later or what?"

Ellie laughed. "You haven't seen ballet dancers at a disco," she said. "We're terrible. About as un-funky as you can get. You can teach me, right?"

Phoebe linked arms with Ellie as they walked out of the registry office to the hotel next door, where the reception was taking place. "It's good to see you again," she said.

"You too," Ellie said warmly. "Really, really good."

After lunch and some funny speeches from Steve and his best man, the music started and everybody got up to dance. Ellie had such fun whirling around with Phoebe and Bethany that she forgot about *The Nutcracker* for a couple of hours.

And then her phone rang. Lara, just as she'd promised.

"How was it? How did you do?" Ellie demanded breathlessly into her cell phone, without even saying hello.

There was an answering chuckle from Lara. "Hello, Ellie, nice to speak to you, too," she said. "Oh, but it was grand. It was the business! I've still got goose bumps! Oh, Ellie, I can't wait for you to do it tomorrow, so you know how great it is. It was so exciting—you're going to love every second of it!"

When the call ended, one of Ellie's favorite tunes began and she caught sight of Phoebe still wiggling on the dance floor with one of Steve's sisters. Ellie danced her way over, feeling as light as air. She was glad Lara had had a good day—because *she* had, too. Even better, it was her turn to dance on stage tomorrow. She just hoped she could dance as well as Lara now. It sounded as if she had an awful lot to live up to!

Phoebe grabbed Ellie's hands and they swung each other around, giggling dizzily. "Happy?" asked Phoebe.

"Very," said Ellie.

Chapter
11

Ellie was backstage, dressed in her scarlet dress and cloak, her makeup expertly applied, and her hair twisted and sprayed into ringlets. She'd wondered before if she'd be feeling nervous at this point but now it had come to it, she just felt dizzy with excitement. As she'd been getting ready, an enormous bunch of flowers had come from Mom and Steve for her, plus good-luck calls from Phoebe and Bethany on her cell phone.

She thought about the audience filing into their seats, rustling their programs, chatting expectantly about the show. She'd heard the strains of the orchestra tuning up in the pit, front of stage. And now here she was with the rest of the cast, about to dance at The Royal Opera House for real!

Ellie's heart was pounding. *Any minute now*, she kept telling herself, *I'll be skipping onto that stage behind Jessica. I'll be dancing with The Royal Ballet!*

Matt elbowed her from behind. "Break a leg," he whispered.

"I hope not," Ellie groaned. "That would be just my luck!"

"No, idiot, I meant—" he laughed.

"I know," Ellie said. "I was just kidding. I—"

"Here we go," Jessica muttered suddenly. "We're on."

Ellie, Matt, Justin, Jessica, and all of the others danced onto the stage as the party children, to be greeted by Clara's grandparents. The stage lights were so dazzlingly bright that, for a second, Ellie felt, with a sickening lurch, that she couldn't see where she was going.

There was Daniel, one of the Year 11 boys, as the butler who had to take all of their cloaks. Each of the children gave him their cloak and *pirouetted* away. Ellie took a deep breath as she passed her cloak to Daniel, and then spun away lightly, her heart pounding. She'd done it!

Meanwhile, Daniel, the butler, was gradually getting overwhelmed by the pile of cloaks and pantomiming panic. Ellie felt herself start to relax as she heard a few chuckles from the audience. So far, so good!

Once all the guests had taken off their cloaks, the children were called into the parlor to receive their gifts and watch the lighting of the Christmas tree. It was Ellie's favorite part of the ballet. As the sweet music swelled around them and the first twinkling lights went on, she found that she had tears in her eyes, thinking back to being that little girl who'd watched *The Nutcracker* on stage so many years ago. She remembered how she'd thought at the time how wonderful it would be to be a party guest for real.

And here I am, she thought with a rush of happiness. *And I was right. It is wonderful. It's the best feeling ever!*

•　　　•　　　•　　　•

The rest of the performance seemed to go by in a blur. It was such fun to dance in front of such a huge audience, knowing that somewhere out there were Mom and Steve, Gran and Gramps, Phoebe and Bethany with their moms too, all watching her. She wondered how many little girls were there, watching her as well, longing to be on stage, just as she'd done all those years ago. It was a magical feeling.

Before she knew it, it was the end of the show. The thunder of applause was deafening. Ellie's legs felt like jelly with excitement and for a moment, she didn't think she'd be able to walk back on stage for the curtain call. But there she stood in a line with Matt and the other party children, bowing with the rest of the company. And still the applause wasn't slowing! It couldn't *just* be her mom doing all the clapping, could it?!

Somehow, her wobbly legs carried her off the stage again. And there was Lara, waiting in the wings for her, her face wreathed in smiles. "Ellie Brown, you are a star," she said, giving Ellie a big hug. "You did it!"

"I did," Ellie said, feeling dazed and overwhelmed. She hugged Lara back. "And so did you. We're both stars."

"I'm so glad I stayed," Lara said. "Thank you, Ellie."

Ellie looked into her friend's shining eyes and smiled. "You're welcome," she said. "I'm glad you stayed, too."

Dear Diary,

I danced with The Royal Ballet on stage at The Royal Opera House tonight! Me, Ellie, regular kid from Chicago. No, I can't believe it either. Any moment now, somebody is going to wake me up. I felt like I was dancing through the most wonderful dream—the best dream of my life.

It was so awesome! I loved it, every single minute of the show. And to think I'm going to do it all over—again and again!

Oh, life is so fantastic! I truly feel like I am the luckiest girl in the world. What an amazing first term I've had at The Royal Ballet Lower School. I can hardly wait to see what's going to happen in the second term!

Signing off—absolutely starving after all that showbiz and glamour!

Party child Number 3—Ellie Brown

About
The Royal Ballet School

A BRIEF HISTORY

The Royal Ballet School enjoys worldwide recognition as a renowned institution for classical ballet training. Its Royal Charter, linking it with the Royal Ballet Companies, assures its purpose and its commitment to excellence.

The founding of the school came in 1926, when Dame Ninette de Valois opened her Academy of Choreographic Art. Inspired to create a repertory ballet company and school, she collaborated with Lilian Baylis, lessee and Manager of the Old Vic Theatre. When Lilian Baylis acquired the Sadler's Wells Theatre, de Valois moved the School there in 1931 and it became The Vic-Wells Ballet School, feeding dancers into The Vic-Wells Ballet Company. In 1939 the school was re-named The Sadler's Wells Ballet School and the Company became The Sadler's Wells Ballet.

In 1946 The Sadler's Wells Ballet moved to a permanent home at the Royal Opera House, Covent Garden. A second company was formed, The Sadler's Wells Theatre Ballet. In 1947 the School moved from Sadler's Wells Theatre to Barons Court and general education was, at last, combined with vocational ballet training.

The Lower School moved to White Lodge, Richmond Park, in 1955/56 and became residential, combining general education and vocational ballet training. The Upper School remained at Barons Court.

The Royal Charter was granted in October 1956 and the

School and companies were renamed The Royal Ballet School, The Royal Ballet, and the Sadler's Wells Royal Ballet (later renamed Birmingham Royal Ballet following its move there in 1990).

From that time, the School has become both the leading classical ballet school in the United Kingdom earning government support and an international institution that attracts the very best ballet students worldwide. The caliber of students graduating from the school is self-evident. Previous Royal Ballet School students include: Dame Margot Fonteyn, Sir Kenneth MacMillan, Sir Peter Wright, Dame Antoinette Sibley, Sir Anthony Dowell, Dame Merle Park, Monica Mason OBE, Lynn Seymour, Marcia Haydee, Jiri Kylian, David Wall, Lesley Collier CBE, Wayne Eagling, Stephen Jefferies, Marion Tait CBE, David Bintley CBE, Leanne Benjamin, Darcey Bussell OBE, Alina Cojocaru, Miyako Yoshida, Adam Cooper, Jonathan Cope CBE, Christopher Hampson, Kevin O'Hare, Ivan Putrov, and Christopher Wheeldon.

In January 2003 the Upper School moved to new premises in Floral Street, alongside London's Royal Opera House in Covent Garden. The state of the art studios are linked to The Royal Ballet by the award winning Bridge of Aspiration thus fulfilling Madam's dream to have Company and School side by side in the center of London.

Through its widespread, comprehensive "Search for Talent" program, the school ensures that children with a gift for dance, a physique suitable for classical ballet, and a motivation to perform are discovered at a young age and nurtured through their formative years.

MISSION AND PURPOSE

The Royal Ballet School's mission is to train and educate outstanding classical ballet dancers for The Royal Ballet, Birmingham Royal Ballet, and other top international dance companies, and in doing so to set the standards in dance training, nationally and internationally.

The School offers an eight-year carefully structured dance course, aligned with an extensive academic program, giving the students the best possible education to equip them for a career in the world of dance.

THE SCHOOL'S GOALS ARE TO:

• Provide, in a caring environment, artistic and academic training of the highest possible caliber, offering all students of the School a positive learning experience that is constantly monitored for potential improvement
• Achieve recognized accreditation for the vocational curriculum
• Offer students as many performing opportunities as possible
• Ensure that the students have close practical and artistic access to Royal Ballet companies

- Maintain a high employment rate of graduating dancers, with many being recruited to The Royal Ballet or Birmingham Royal Ballet
- Expand the international exposure of the students of the School by participating in international competitions and festivals
- Develop new state-of-the-art, purpose built facilities that will enhance the teaching and learning opportunities for the students
- Conduct an extensive Audition and Outreach program

WHITE LODGE

Many of the new pupils arriving at White Lodge each year have been there before—to summer school, for instance—but nothing can match the excitement of knowing that a new chapter in one's life has opened.

Pupils come from many backgrounds, and there is no sense of anyone being different. But there is a strong feeling of history—White Lodge is nearly three hundred years old—that one feels walking through the front door and into the Ballet Museum!

The pupils have to work hard, but they share the feeling of a sense of purpose gained by studying alongside others with common goals. Everyone wants to be there, studying at White Lodge, and everyone wants to succeed.

The workday is long and physically tiring, but it is organized so that students can have a balanced life: homework, music practice, rehearsals, and even free time all have their place. As in any boarding school (and just like at home!) meal times and bed times are regulated during the week but are more flexible on weekends. Weekend visitors to White Lodge will find pupils playing tennis, attending a debate, developing photographs, watching television, or simply relaxing in the dorms. In other words, being normal kids!

Students never forget their years at White Lodge. For the aspiring young dancer, it is simply the place to be. Even for those who don't eventually become professional dancers, it is the experience of a lifetime: a happy, fulfilled community of like-minded individuals growing up in a sympathetic environment.

The stuff of dreams!

"Life in the school is like being part of a large family because everyone is close to each other and grow up together so much. We all respect each other and this produces wonderful friendships."—year 10 pupil (1997)

CURRICULUM

Pupils at White Lodge have a balanced curriculum that leads ultimately to Year 11, in which they audition for entry to the Upper School, and must quickly adjust to taking dance courses throughout the day in between "regular" classes in general studies. The day begins at 8:30 a.m. There are three two-hour blocks of time during the day, lasting until 4 p.m., filled with one two-hour ballet class and six academic lessons.

During ballet class, students are expected to go "back to

basics," working slowly and methodically and mastering each stage before moving on. Boys and girls each have their own dance classes.

Academic classes are taught by subject specialists, and new subjects abound, including drama, information technology, French, and religion.

Many more dance classes take place in the late afternoon and early evening. And there are rehearsals—for School performances but also to work with The Royal Ballet itself.

All pupils have dance classes on Saturdays, but by lunchtime can usually go home or stay at White Lodge to enjoy a communal weekend.

Boarding school may be an adjustment for some students, but it is rare for a pupil not to be able to cope with life at White Lodge. After all, it's not all work—there are sports, indoor games, hobbies, shopping, spending time with friends, watching television—just like home, really!

PERFORMANCE

To dance onstage is every pupil's ambition. Even if it only happens once in a lifetime, it's a dream come true. This is what all of the training is for, what it's about.

Pupils at The Royal Ballet School have performance built into their lives. Performance in front of their peers, learning their craft step by step.

And also in front of over two thousand eager ballet lovers in the audience at the Royal Opera House in Covent Garden! Sometimes first-year pupils at White Lodge are given the chance to perform in their very first term, when they are allowed to audition for The Royal Ballet's *Nutcracker* at Christmas, or Matthew Hart's *Peter and the Wolf*, specially choreographed for the School Performance in 1995 and since then a regular feature in The Royal Ballet's repertoire.

But not all performance is so highly exposed. White Lodge pupils perform for their parents, their previous ballet teachers, and to the many visitors to the School. During the summer they give their own special outdoor performances of folk dancing and other disciplines to a wider public—at White Lodge and elsewhere. And to special friends, such as the terminally ill care at Trinity Hospice.

Pupils compete for choreographic prizes, too, as do Upper School students, in the annual Ursula Moreton Choreographic Competition. Many work with The Royal Ballet, Birmingham Royal Ballet, and occasionally other companies during their graduation year, which therefore becomes a busy time.

And it's not just dance that is performed: Recent School Concerts have included Berlioz's *Requiem*, Orff's *Carmina Burana*, and Stravinsky's *Les Noces* sung by the whole school. White Lodge pupils compete in an annual Music Competition and put on dramatic performances. Nerves? Not these pupils!

LIFE AFTER THE ROYAL BALLET SCHOOL

Graduating students have learned their craft as dancers, practiced it as performers, achieved significant academic success, and grown into mature young adults.

The majority of students who have completed the Dancer's Course obtain posts as dancers in classical ballet companies on graduation from the School. Many join The Royal Ballet and Birmingham Royal Ballet, both of which take the majority of their corps de ballet entrants from the school.

Entry to the two Royal Ballet companies is not by formal audition: The Company Directors watch the Graduate class students frequently and assess their progress. Many students work with one or the other of the two Royal Ballet companies during their Graduate year, a chance for both the Company and the student to judge the suitability of any eventual employment opportunity.

Directors of many other ballet companies come to the School to watch classes. In some cases, they may conduct a formal audition. Students are made aware of auditions being held by companies throughout the UK and Europe during the year and are encouraged to attend those that are suitable.

To learn more about The Royal Ballet School, please visit their website at:
www.royalballetschool.co.uk

GLOSSARY

ROYAL BALLET METHOD: An eight-year system of training and methodology developed and utilized by The Royal Ballet School to produce dancers with clean, pure classical technique

ARABESQUE: One leg is extended to the back (the name is taken from the flourished, curved line used in Arabic motifs)

BALANCE(S): To rock; a swinging three-step movement transferring weight from one foot to the other

BARRE: The horizontal wooden bar fastened to the walls of the ballet classroom or rehearsal hall that the dancer holds for support

BATTEMENT(S): To beat; a beating of the legs; see *grand battement* and *petit battement* for variations

BRAS BAS: The rounding of the arms held in front of the thighs with a small space between the hands

CHASSÉ(S)/ *also* PAS CHASSÉ(S): A gliding step when the leg slides out and the other leg is drawn along the floor to it

COUP DE PIED: Around the "neck" of the foot; one pointed foot is placed at the calf—just above the ankle—of the opposite leg

CROISÉ: To cross (in which the dancer faces the audience diagonally and has one leg crossed in front of the other)

DEMI-PLIÉ: A small bend (of the knees) in alignment over the toes, without causing the heel, or heels, of the foot to lift off the floor

DEVELOPPÉ: The unfolding of the working leg; the leg is drawn to the knee and then extended from there

ECHAPPÉ(S): To escape (a movement that begins in 5th position and moves quickly to 2nd position either by sliding feet to the ball of the foot or as a jump from 5th position to 2nd position)

FONDU(S): To melt (bending and extending of the legs at the same time with one leg supporting the body)

FOUETTE(S): To whip; a quick movement on one leg that requires the dancer to change direction and can be performed in a variety of ways

GLISSADE: To glide; a connecting step that begins and ends in *plié*

GRAND BATTEMENT: A throwing action of the fully extended leg in any direction with controlled lowering

GRAND PLIÉ: A deeper bend (of the knees) bringing the heels of the feet off the floor

PAS DE CHATS: Cat's step (because the movement is like a cat's leap); a jump where the legs are lifted and lowered separately, forming a diamond shape in the air

PAS DE BOURRÉE: A linking movement done as a series of three quick small steps

PETIT BATTEMENT: Small beat whereby a pointed foot "beats" in front and back of the calf—just above the ankle—of the opposite leg; this exercise is done with great rapidity

PIROUETTE: Turn (used to describe a turn, whirl, or spin); sometimes referred to "turns" as *tours*

PLIÉ(S): To bend (the knee or knees)

POINTE: "Going on *pointe*" is to graduate from soft ballet shoes to the more demanding *pointe* shoes that have been stiffened with shellac (a glue) and allows the ballerina to balance her entire body weight on the tiny flat surface of the shoes

RELEVÉ(S): To rise (used to describe a rise from the whole foot to *demi-pointe* or full *pointe*)

RETIRÉ: Withdrawn (drawing up of the working foot to under the knee)

REVERENCE: A deep curtsey; performed at the end of class, as a mark of thanks and respect

SAUTÉS: To jump off the ground with both feet

SISSONE(S): A scissor-like movement where the dancer jumps from two feet to one foot or two feet to two feet

TEMPS LEVÉ: Raised movement; a sharp jump on one foot

TENDUS: Stretched; held-out; tight (in which a leg is extended straight out to the front *devant*, back *derrière*, or side *à la seconde*, with the foot fully pointed)